the further adventures of

SHERLOCK HOLMES

DR. JEKYLL AND MR. HOLMES

DR. JEKYLL AND MR. HOLMES

LOREN D. ESTLEMAN

TITAN BOOKS

THE FURTHER ADVENTURES OF SHERLOCK HOLMES:
DR. JEKYLL AND MR. HOLMES
ISBN: 9781848567474

Published by
Titan Books
A division of Titan Publishing Group Ltd
144 Southwark St
London
SE1 0UP

First edition: October 2010
10 9 8 7 6 5 4 3 2 1

Visit our website:
www.titanbooks.com

What did you think of this book? We love to hear from our readers. Please email us at: readerfeedback@titanemail.com, or write to us at the above address. To receive advance information, news, competitions, and exclusive Titan offers online, please sign up for the Titan newsletter on our website: www.titanbooks.com

A CIP catalogue record for this title is available from the British Library.

Printed and bound in the USA.

To Sir Arthur Conan Doyle and Robert Louis Stevenson
– one thrill in return for many

"When a doctor goes wrong, he is the first of criminals."
– Sherlock Holmes, as quoted in
"The Adventure of the Speckled Band"

Foreword

"You the guy that did the book about Sherlock Holmes?"

Ordinarily I make it a point to answer that kind of query with an appropriate wisecrack, but there was something about this particular visitor that warned me to keep a leash on my devastating wit. He had emerged from the back seat of a black limousine nearly as long as my driveway, flanked by a pair of healthy-looking young men with jaws like pigs' knuckles and odd bulges beneath the armpits of their tailor-made suits. The fellow in the middle was short and built like a bouncer and had thick black hair in which the marks of his comb glistened beneath the illumination of my porch light. His face was evenly tanned, clean-shaven, and dominated by a pair of solid black wraparound sunglasses, although the sun had long since descended. He looked forty but turned out later to be closer to sixty. When he spoke, he had a Brooklyn accent that dared me to sneer at it. I didn't.

"I edited *The Adventure of the Sanguinary Count,* if that's what you mean," said I. I was determined in spite of his formidable appearance to remain master of the situation. His visit had interrupted my writing and I was anxious to get back to it.

Without turning his head he held out a hand to the young man at his right, who immediately placed in it a package wrapped in brown paper, which he then thrust into my hands.

"Read it," he ordered.

I opened my mouth to protest, but the eyes of his companions grew cold suddenly, and instead I stepped aside from the door to admit the trio. Once inside, the man in the middle took possession of my favorite easy chair while the others took up standing positions on either side of it, quiet and solid as andirons. I glanced longingly toward the telephone, but my chances of reaching it and dialing for help before one of them showed me what the lumps were in their jackets and pumped me full of lead were less than encouraging, and in any case if this was a robbery or a kidnapping, it was being handled in such a bizarre manner that as a writer I thought it might be worth my while to see it through. All three watched as I sat down on the sofa opposite them and opened the package.

I had all I could do to refrain from groaning when I read the title. Since the publication of *Sherlock Holmes vs. Dracula: Or the Adventure of the Sanguinary Count*, of which I was the editor, I had become the recipient of no fewer than three "genuine" Watsonian manuscripts sent to me from scattered corners of the world. I had not required an expert to tell me that none of them was worth the paper it had been forged upon. Nor had I use for another. Faced, however, with a most persuasive argument in the persons of the three strapping fellows in my living room, I read on.

A fresh glance at the handwriting caused my pulse to quicken. I had spent too much time decoding Watson's earlier manuscript not to recognize his careless scrawl when I encountered it again. It was written on ancient vellum, with many corrections in the margins – signs of the Victorian perfectionist which were usually lost when A. Conan Doyle, his friend and literary agent, copied out his works for publication. I was immediately convinced of its authenticity. Quite forgetting my "guests," I continued reading and finished the manuscript in that one sitting. When I set it aside some three hours later I was burning with curiosity, but I managed to appear casual as I asked the fellow in the dark glasses how the artifact had come into his possession. The story he told bears repeating.

In 1943, while serving a five-year penitentiary sentence for armed robbery, my visitor, who gave his name as Georgie Collins (a pseudonym; I was better off, he said, not knowing his real identity), was approached by the U.S. Army and offered the chance to shorten his term if he joined the service. He accepted, and a year later found himself in France during the post-D-Day Allied offensive.

One day he and a small patrol stormed a bombed-out chateau near Toulouse, "blew away" a nest of Germans hidden inside, and set to work searching the rubble for much-needed supplies. In a space between two walls Collins spotted a tattered sheaf of papers, covered with dust and bound with a faded black ribbon. After reading only a few lines he saw the discovery for what it was and, making sure that none of his colleagues was observing him, tucked the manuscript away inside his rucksack.

Surreptitiously questioning the locals, Collins learned that the chateau had been used for medical research by Doctor, later Sir, John H. Watson when he served as a civilian attached to the British Army during the First World War. The area had been heavily shelled even then; it seemed likely that during one of these bombardments the manuscript had been dislodged from the top of a table or bureau and had fallen through a hole in the wall and been left behind in the confusion of the final days of the war.

History repeated itself. Shortly after his return to the States, Georgie

Collins married his childhood sweetheart and tossed the rucksack containing the manuscript into a utility closet in his home, where it lay forgotten among his other war mementos for more than three decades. If not for the popularity of the other lost work which I had edited, he said, it might still be there.

When I asked him why he had come to me, Collins smiled for the first time. He had very white teeth, very even – the work, no doubt, of an expensive cosmetic dentist.

"I got a sudden need for cash," he said. "When I heard about this here Sherlock Holmes book you did, I remembered that thing I found in France and figured you might be willing to do whatever it is you do with these things and split the take with me. I don't know nothing about editing. The only editor I ever knew got blew up in his car when he tried to publish a piece about an acquaintance of mine."

I explained to him that profits are a long time coming in the publishing business and asked if he was prepared to wait several months for his share. The smile fled from his features.

"I ain't got that kind of time. How much can you give me right now, tonight?"

"How much do you want?"

The figure he quoted had too many zeros. I countered with one of my own. His frown grew dangerous. Sensing his displeasure, the men beside his chair perked up like dogs anticipating the signal to attack.

"Chicken feed," he snarled.

I summoned up my courage and shrugged. "It's most of what I own. I need something to live on. You can consider it a down payment."

He scratched his chin noisily. "All right, I'll take it. In cash."

"I don't have that much on hand. Will you take a check?" I reached for my checkbook.

"I only deal in cash."

"I'll have to go to the bank, and it won't be open again until Monday."

He fidgeted in his chair, made faces. Finally: "Okay, I'll take the check. Make it out to cash."

I did so, and handed it to him. "It's good," I said as he studied it closely.

"I believe you." He folded the check and put it away inside his coat. "You don't look that dumb."

My writer's curiosity got the better of me and I asked him why he needed the money in such a hurry. To my surprise, he seemed unruffled by the question.

"Travel expenses. Some people are looking for me, and some others don't want me found. So I'm taking a vacation. Every cent I got is tied up in the — in my business." He got up and stood looking down at me. The lamplight glinted off the opaque lenses of his glasses. "Do a good job with it. You'll be hearing from me again soon."

He turned upon his heel and left, but not before one of the young men, slipping his hand inside his jacket, leaned out through the doorway, glanced to right and left, then straightened and nodded to his chief. The three went out together. A moment later I heard the engine of the limousine purr into life, then a crunch of gravel as it swept into the road and was gone. By that time I had already snatched up a pencil and set to work.

The prospect of editing this manuscript presented much the same difficulties as I had experienced with the first. I have established that Watson's handwriting was abominable; worse, the existence of a surprising number of redundancies and mixed metaphors made it abundantly clear that this was a first draft and that much revising was necessary before it could be allowed to go to the typesetters — revising which, possibly because of the war and the subsequent misplacing of the manuscript, Watson was unable to accomplish. I have, therefore, taken it upon myself to provide those corrections which I am certain the good doctor would have supplied had not time and circumstances been working against him. I am prepared to take the consequences for this literary blasphemy, with the understanding that wherever possible I have left Watson's prose untouched, and that where this was not possible I have endeavored to keep to his distinctive style. The book, then, is ninety per cent original.

The narrative provides two significant revelations which may or may not clear up a number of outstanding arguments among Sherlockians, depending upon how they are received. First, the appearance of Sherlock Holmes's brother Mycroft in 1885 would indicate that Watson, writing of his first meeting with the elder Holmes in "The Greek Interpreter," was guilty of literary license. Since this initial encounter would of necessity predate the events contained herein, it was impossible for Mycroft to have said, upon being introduced, "I hear of Sherlock everywhere since you became his chronicler." As every student knows, the first of these chronicles, *A Study in Scarlet*, did not appear until December of 1887, more than two years after the events described in the present account. If Mycroft did indeed make that statement, he would have had to have done so on some later occasion. This is not so difficult to accept, as Watson was sometimes known to telescope conversations made on different occasions into one in order to make his account more complete. A case in point: Watson asserts, in "The Final Problem," that he has "never" heard of the evil Professor Moriarty when in fact, as we are shown in *The Valley of Fear*, which predates that account, he is already fairly well informed upon the subject. Since "Problem" appeared first, the good doctor obviously chose to include Holmes's introductory description of the wicked scholar from some earlier occasion in order not to confuse his readers, who were unaware of the professor's existence. This same reasoning may account for Mycroft's opening lines in "The Greek Interpreter," a case which we now see had to have taken place prior to January of 1885.

Second, we are at last made aware of Watson's *alma mater*, the University of Edinburgh, where he studied medicine before taking his degree at the University of London in 1878. The subject has long been a controversial one among erudite Sherlockians, who, knowing that the London facility of Watson's day was not a teaching institution but merely a clearinghouse of diplomas, have spent many hours arguing over where Holmes's Boswell attended classes. Perhaps it is there that he met Conan Doyle prior to the latter's graduation from the same university in 1881 and sowed the seeds for the working relationship which was to make the name of Sherlock Holmes synonymous with the art of detection.

The following, with some slight interference of my own, is a chronicle in Watson's own words of the period between October 1883 and March 1885 – hitherto a Sherlockian mystery – and of those events connected with the bizarre relationship of Henry Jekyll to Edward Hyde as viewed from a fresh angle. Whether or not, as in the case of their brush with Count Dracula in 1890, the part played by Holmes and Watson had any effect upon its outcome will likely remain a point of debate among scholars for some time to come. In my opinion it was the Baker Street sleuth's bloodhound tenacity which forced Mr. Hyde to live up to his name.

As for Georgie Collins, I was to hear of him again sooner than either of us expected. Two days after our parting I read in the newspaper of the death of a reputed underworld chief who had been gunned down that morning along with his two bodyguards at Detroit Metropolitan Airport. He had been sought by a grand jury investigating the mysterious disappearance of a famed labor leader, and it was believed that he had been silenced by his gangland cronies. Found upon his person was a one-way ticket to Mexico and a substantial amount of cash worn in a money belt. A photograph identified as one taken of the victim two years before, during his trial for income tax evasion, showed my visitor of the other night handcuffed between two gray-looking federal agents. Although the name beneath the picture was different, there was no mistaking the hard white smile he was flashing. Only the sunglasses were missing.

Whatever his sins, and however base his motives, Georgie Collins is responsible for the present volume's existence; because of this, his place among the great literary patrons of history is assured. I will therefore take the risk of official disapproval by dedicating this Foreword to his memory.

Loren D. Estleman
Dexter, Michigan
December 15, 1978

Preface

One might think, now that the world is falling down about our ears, that interest in a man whose entire career was with few exceptions dedicated to the eradication of domestic evils would naturally diminish in the face of danger from without. That, however, is not the case. My publishers have for some time been badgering me to dip once again into that battered tin dispatch-box in which I long ago packed away the last of my notes dealing with those singular problems which engaged the gifts of Mr. Sherlock Holmes, and to lay yet another of them before an eager public. For a long time I demurred – not because of any unwillingness upon my part but rather in deference to the wishes of my friend, who has since his retirement repeatedly enjoined me from taking any action to enhance fame which has of late proved cumbersome to him. The reader may imagine my reaction then, when, one day last week, I answered the telephone in my Kensington home and recognised Sherlock Holmes's voice upon the line.

'Good morning, Watson. I trust that you are well.'

'Holmes!'

'Whose call were you anticipating so anxiously, or does that fall under the heading of "most secret"?'

My surprise at being made contact with in this fashion by one for whom the telegraph remained the chief form of communication was heightened by this unexpected and accurate observation.

'How did you know that I was expecting a telephone call?' I asked incredulously.

'Simplicity itself. You answered the infernal device before the first ring was completed.'

'Wonderful! But what brings you to London? I thought that you had retired to the South Downs, this time for good.'

'I am seeing a specialist about my rheumatism. I am afraid that the two years I spent trailing Von Bork did me no service. Have you still in your possession your notes regarding the affair in Soho in '84?'

I was caught off-guard by this seeming irrelevancy. 'Indeed I do,' I responded.

'Excellent. I think that your readers may find some interest in the complete account. Mind you, be kind to Stevenson.'

'The legal question –'

'– is moot, I think, after all these years. Whitehall has far more important things to deal with at present than a thirty-year-old shooting, particularly one committed in self-defence.'

From there he steered the conversation into a discussion of the progress of the war, agreed with me that America's entry into the conflict would spell doom for the Huns, and rang off after a talk of less than three minutes.

Since I have never pretended to any talents in detection, I shall not attempt to fathom his reason for dragging forth this long-buried memory, which would seem to hold little in common with the holocaust in which Europe finds itself at present. I had asked for and been denied permission to publish the facts of that case too many times to question this unexpected boon. To borrow a phrase from the Yanks, I am not inclined towards looking gift horses in the mouth; I shall, therefore, make haste to consult my notebook for the years 1883-85, set down the events as they occurred at the time, and concern myself with my friend's state of mind upon some other occasion.

Holmes's admonition to 'be kind to Stevenson' was unnecessary. Although it is true that Robert Louis Stevenson's account of the singular circumstances surrounding the murder of Sir Danvers Carew contains numerous omissions, it is just as true that discretion, and not slovenliness, obliged him to withhold certain facts and to publish *The Strange Case of Dr. Jekyll and Mr. Hyde* under the guise of fiction. Victorian society simply would not have accepted it in any other form.

Now, after thirty-two years, the full story can at last be told. The pages which follow this preface represent variations upon the theme set forth in Stevenson's largely accurate but incomplete account. As with any two differing points of view, some details, particularly those dealing with time, vary, although not significantly. This is due, no doubt, to the fact that my notes were made upon first-hand observation at the time the events were unfolding, whilst Stevenson's were made upon hearsay at best, months and in some cases years after the fact. I leave the decision concerning whose version is correct to the reader.

As I write these words, it occurs to me that the story is in fact a timely one, in that it demonstrates the evils which a science left to itself may inflict upon an unsuspecting mankind. A culture which allows zeppelins to rain death and destruction upon the cities of men and heavy guns to pound civilisation back into the dust whence it came is a culture which has yet to learn from its mistakes. It is therefore hoped that the chronicle which follows will serve as a lesson to the world that the laws of nature are inviolate, and that the penalty for any attempt to circumvent them is swift and merciless. Assuming, that is, that there will still be a world when the present cataclysm has run its course

John H. Watson, M.D.
London, England
August 6th, 1917.

One

THE MYSTERIOUS BENEFICIARY

'Holmes,' said I, 'I have a cab waiting.'

I was standing in the doorway of our lodgings at 221B Baker Street, hands in the pockets of my ulster and glad of its warmth now that the chill of late October had begun to invade the sitting-room in the absence of a fire in the grate. My fellow-lodger, however, appeared oblivious to the cold as he busied himself at the acid-stained deal table in the corner, his long, thin back concealing from me his specific operations. Nearby, studying the proceedings in baffled fascination, stood a broad-shouldered commissionaire in the trim uniform of his occupation.

'One moment, Watson,' said Sherlock Holmes, and executed a quarter-turn round upon his stool so that I might see what he was doing. With the aid of a glass pipette he drew a quantity of bluish liquid from a beaker boiling atop the flame of his Bunsen burner and expelled it into a test tube which he held in his left hand. Then he laid aside the pipette and took up a slip of paper upon which was heaped a small mound of white powder, curling it part way round his thumb so as not to spill any of its contents. His metallic grey eyes were bright with anticipation.

'Purple is the fatal colour, Doctor,' he informed me. 'Should the liquid assume that hue once I have introduced this other substance – as I suspect it will – a murder has been committed and a woman will march to the gallows. Thus!' He tipped the powder into the tube.

The commissionaire and I leant forward to stare at the contents. The powder formed curling patterns as it descended through the liquid, but long before it reached the bottom it dissolved. In its place, a stream of bright bubbles sped to the top and floated there. Holmes drummed the table with impatient fingers, awaiting the expected result.

The liquid retained its bluish tint.

I am not by nature an envious person, and yet, as moment followed upon moment with no change in the colour of the concoction in the tube, I confess that I had all I could do to maintain my countenance in the presence of Holmes's undisguised bewilderment. He seemed so invariably right that I can scarcely describe the elation which I as a mere mortal felt to witness a rare moment of fallibility upon his part, proving that he, too, was subject to the frailties of the race. Fortunately for our relationship, my efforts to control my own mirth became unnecessary when he burst out laughing.

'Well, well,' said he, once he had recaptured his customary calm, 'so the matter is an innocent one after all, and the joke is on me. Well, it's a hazard of the profession, this *penchant* for always looking towards the dark side; if nothing else, I have learnt a most valuable lesson.' He replaced the test tube in its rack, took up a pen and a scrap of paper, scribbled something upon the latter, and handed the message and a coin to the commissionaire. 'Take this to Inspector Gregson, my good man, and tell him that Mr. Wingate Dennis did indeed die a natural death – as the postmortem will undoubtedly reveal – and that Mrs. Dennis is guilty of no more heinous a crime than a perhaps too free use of sugar in her husband's tea. And now, Watson,' said he, as the messenger departed, 'it's you and me for King's Cross Station and the North of England for a well-deserved rest.' He rose from the stool and reached for his hat and coat.

During the early years of our friendship preceding my marriage, and even before I had begun to chronicle our adventures together, Sherlock Holmes's fame as a consulting detective had travelled by word-of-mouth throughout London, and people in distress were turning to him for aid in such volumes that by the autumn of 1883 I became seriously concerned for his health and demanded that he take a holiday. This time, to my surprise – for I had made much the same suggestion upon a number of occasions and been turned down – he readily agreed, and at last our bags were packed and loaded and we had but to descend to ground level and climb aboard the hansom to be off to Nottingham for a month of relaxation far from the ills of the city. Under the circumstances, the reader may understand my chagrin when, just as we were heading for the door, our landlady came in with a card upon her salver and announced that we had a visitor.

'"G. J. Utterson",' Holmes read, taking up the card. 'Did you explain to Mr. Utterson that we are leaving, Mrs. Hudson?'

'I did, Mr. Holmes, but the gentleman said that his business is urgent.'

'Very well, then, send him up. And please be good enough to ask the cabby to wait a bit longer.' He turned a rueful face upon me. 'I am truly sorry, my dear fellow, but as a doctor you will agree that turning one's back upon a brother human being in need is hardly the act of a responsible practitioner.'

'As a doctor,' said I curtly, 'I can only warn that you are courting grave danger.'

He removed his outer garments and returned them to their hook. 'It is the price I pay for being the only one of my kind. But pray, put up your own coat and hat and prepare to assume your favourite seat, for

I judge by our visitor's troubled footfall that he will welcome an extra pair of sympathetic ears.'

Presently the door opened again and a grave-visaged gentleman was ushered into our quarters. In appearance he was between forty and fifty years of age, leaning towards the latter, and was dressed most impeccably in a dark suit and topcoat with a quiet check. On his boots he sported a pair of neat gaiters, but since these were not in keeping with the soberness of the rest of his attire I gathered that they had been donned more for protection than for style, as a light rain had been falling over London throughout the day and puddles were numerous. I have mentioned that his visage was grave, but as he stepped farther into the light cast by the single lamp we had left burning, the similarities between it and the face of a professional mourner grew sharp. Long, rugged, scored across the brow with creases of worry, it might have belonged to an aged bloodhound but for a modest black moustache and greying hair carefully arranged and pomaded to conceal a balding pate. His eyes too were sad, but with a genuine sorrow that could only have been the result of deepest despair. My heart had never gone out to a complete stranger as swiftly as it went out to Mr. G. J. Utterson even before he opened his mouth to speak.

He waited until Mrs. Hudson had withdrawn, closing the door behind her, then looked from one to the other of us as if uncertain which man to address first.

'Good afternoon, Mr. Utterson,' Holmes opened, offering his hand, which was reservedly accepted. 'I am Sherlock Holmes and this is my companion, Dr. Watson, in whom you may place whatever confidence you extend to me. I shan't ask you to remove your coat – it is, after all, chilly in here without a fire – but there is a chair; I suggest that you take it, for you must be exhausted after walking about London most of the day.'

Our visitor had been in the act of seating himself in the chair which we set aside for prospective clients; at Holmes's final remark he paused in some astonishment, then dropped into it as though weakened by a physical blow. 'However did you ascertain that?' he stammered. 'What you say is true, but I cannot imagine how –'

'Common observation,' interrupted my friend, offering the newcomer a cigar from his case, which was declined. 'Your trousers are liberally splashed with various kinds of mud from different parts of the city. They reach rather higher than they would have had you been traveling in, say, a hansom or a four-wheeler; hence my deduction that you were walking. That you have been doing so for the best part of the day is evident by the variety of the splashes, indicating that you covered a great deal of ground in your meanderings. There is also a dried crust upon the left side of the crown of your hat – precipitated there, most likely, by the hand of some ruffian in the East End, which from the quality of your attire I should judge to be somewhat removed from your usual surroundings.'

Mr. Utterson looked down at the top hat resting upon his knee, the band of which was indeed encrusted with dirt upon one side. 'My hat was dislodged by a handful of mud hurled by a filthy little chimney sweep in Houndsditch, but a wave of my stick put him to flight. In another moment I suppose you will tell me his name.'

'You flatter me beyond my abilities,' said Holmes. But his cheeks flushed at the compliment. He sank into his beloved armchair and stretched his long legs out before the nonexistent fire. 'I should like to hear a statement of your problem, Mr. Utterson, which my landlady informs me is of some moment. I beg you to lay it before me exactly as you would prepare any case for a magistrate. Oh, no more praise, if you please' – here he raised a hand – 'that sheaf of legal documents protruding from your inside breast pocket could only belong to an lawyer. I recognise a telltale Latin phrase here and there among its text.'

At the mention of his profession, our visitor had shot bolt upright, gripping the arms of his chair, but as Holmes explained the simple steps by which he had arrived at his conclusion, he relaxed, though not so completely as he might have done were he at home in his own sitting-room. I knew from prior experience how unsettling it was to be in the presence of a man before whom one's life was an open book.

'If it please you, sir,' he said, 'I think I have use for that cigar which you offered me earlier.'

The case being out of Holmes's reach, I picked it up and pushed it across to the lawyer. He selected a cigar, snipped the end off fastidiously with a silver clipper on the end of his watch-chain, shook his head politely to my offer of a match, and lit it with one of his own.

'Your name, Mr. Holmes, was given me by my cousin, Mr. Richard Enfield, who engaged your services some time ago in a matter involving the disappearance of a rare coin which had been entrusted to his care. He told me that you were a man upon whose confidence I could rely absolutely.'

Holmes caught my eye and wiggled a finger in the direction of his desk. I caught his meaning and, after unlocking and opening the drawer, drew out his small case-book and brought it over to him.

'Thank you, Watson,' said he, flipping through the pages. 'Enfield. Here it is.' He read swiftly and closed the book. 'I remember the case. An 1813 guinea, stamped twice by accident, resulting in a double image of George III. He was holding it for a friend. It was not stolen at all, but merely misplaced. I found it inside the velvet lining of the box in which it was kept.' He held up the book, which I returned to the drawer and locked away. 'Would that all of life's difficulties were as easily resolved, eh, Mr. Utterson?'

The other nodded in grave agreement. 'I fear that the problem which

I bring does not fall into that category.' He leant forward in his chair. 'Please do not think it an insult, but I must stress the value — nay, the necessity — of secrecy in this affair. It must not go beyond this room.'

'You have my promise,' said Holmes.

'And mine,' said I.

Our responses seemed to satisfy him, for he nodded again and sat back, puffing at his cigar.

'My oldest client and dearest friend,' he began, 'is a man by the name of Dr. Henry Jekyll, about whom you may have heard. His name is not unknown among circles both social and scientific.'

'I am familiar with his reputation,' said I.

'Then you know that he has been deemed brilliant by a number of our leading medical journals for the great strides which he has made in that field through his research. He is moreover a decent man, to whom friendship is no idle word but a sacred bond, to be preserved at the cost of life itself. Some time ago, however, he came to me with a most unsettling request having to do with his last will and testament.'

'Excuse me,' broke in the detective. 'How old a man is Dr. Jekyll?'

'He is nearing the half-century mark, as indeed am I.'

'Is that not the age at which a man begins seriously to contemplate his own mortality?'

'It is not his wish to draw up a will which upset me,' said the other. 'Rather, it was the terms which he dictated. Shall I show you the document?' He reached inside his coat and drew forth a packet of papers, which he proceeded to unfold.

'Would you not be betraying a confidence if you did?' asked my friend.

'I would rather be deprived of the privilege to practise law because of an indiscretion than lose a friend as close as Henry Jekyll, for it is for his life that I fear.'

'Then pray, summarise the terms. My Latin grows rustier by the day.'

The lawyer donned a pair of gold-rimmed spectacles to consult the paper which he held in his hands. 'Briefly, they add up to the following: In the event of Henry Jekyll's death, disappearance, or unexplained absence for any period to exceed three calendar months, all of his worldly possessions – some two hundred and fifty thousand pounds sterling – are to pass into the hands of a gentleman by the name of Edward Hyde.' He refolded the document and returned it, along with his spectacles, to his pocket. 'Mr. Holmes, have you ever in your life heard of such terms?'

'They are singular, to say the least. Who is this Edward Hyde?'

'That is the mystery which has brought me to you. I never heard of the man before Jekyll named him as beneficiary.'

'You questioned Jekyll?'

'He said only that he had a special interest in the young man. I could draw him out no further.'

'Is that all the information you can supply?'

'There is a second part to my story. I mentioned my cousin, Richard Enfield, earlier. He is a gadabout and something of a gossip, but I find his company refreshing after hours of seclusion with dry paperwork. It was during our constitutional a week ago Sunday that he related to me the details of an incident which have left me virtually sleepless these past eleven nights.

'He told me that he was on his way home from some revel in the wee hours of a winter morning when he chanced to witness a collision involving two pedestrians at a nearby corner. One, a little, dwarf-like man, was hurrying along towards the corner whilst the other, a very young girl, was running at top speed at right angles to him, neither being aware of the other's presence until the moment of impact. It was a commonplace occurrence; a blustering apology would usually ensue if the man was a gentleman, or, if he was not, a sharp word – one could hardly expect more. But the girl fell, and before she could get to her feet this brute trampled right over her, oblivious to her cries and proceeding as if she were the merest pile of debris round which he had not the time to walk. A shocking scene, as Enfield described it.'

'I should say so!' I blurted out, unable to control my reaction to such uncivilised behaviour in the age of Victoria.

Utterson continued, ignoring my comment. 'The ruffian might have escaped, for his pace was swift, but Enfield's stride was longer and he collared him at the corner. By that time the girl's family had arrived and the local physician was summoned, and though by God's grace the child was unharmed, their anger was such that they might have fallen upon the offender and torn him to pieces then and there had not my cousin held them back through sheer force of reason. This was more out of respect for human life upon his part than from any sympathy towards the ruffian, who seemed to inspire a strange revulsion in whoever glimpsed his face beneath the lamplight, including Enfield himself. A blackguard of the most obvious sort, this fellow, was the impression I got.

'In lieu of his life, or at the very least a session in court, the ruffian agreed to surrender the sum of a hundred pounds to the girl's family, and led them presently to the door of a shabby building on a by-street in one of the city's busier quarters, whereupon he asked his escort to wait whilst he produced a key and went in. Some moments later he returned with a purse containing ten pounds in gold and a cheque for the balance, drawn upon the account of a man well known to Enfield. Of course they didn't trust it, so at the ruffian's suggestion they spent the night in my cousin's chambers until the bank opened in the morning and they were able to cash the cheque without incident. After which the fellow was released.'

'An ugly episode,' said Holmes, 'but hardly illuminating. What is its connexion with the matter which we are discussing?'

'The strangest, Mr. Holmes.' Utterson chewed the end of his cigar nervously. It was plain that he was keeping himself in check with an effort. 'When the story was told to me, we were standing across the street from the very door through which the ruffian had passed to fetch the money and the cheque. Enfield pointed it out. It is a side entrance to the home of Dr. Henry Jekyll, and the cheque was made out upon his account to the order of the bearer, Edward Hyde.'

'Good Lord!' I cried.

Holmes, who had listened to Utterson's story thus far in the somnolent attitude which he assumed whenever the facts of a new case were stated to him, sat up suddenly, steely eyes flashing. For the space of a heartbeat he and the lawyer stared at each Other in silence.

'Dismiss the cab, Watson,' said Holmes finally.

SHERLOCK HOLMES ACCEPTS A CASE

Protest upon my part was out of the question. I knew my friend too well to waste breath attempting to divert him from the path down which his natural inclination had led him; instead, I went downstairs, persuaded the burly cab driver to help me carry our bags back up to our rooms, and sent him on his way with a half-sovereign for his troubles. By that time Holmes had kindled a cheery fire in the grate and relieved Utterson of his coat and hat, pausing along the way to pour the lawyer a draught of our very best port. Our visitor tasted it, but it might as well have been the coarsest ale for all the enjoyment he appeared to derive from it. Having thus seen to his guest's needs, Holmes remained standing and began poking shag into the bowl of his cherry-wood pipe with such industry that one might have thought it the most important activity which he had yet undertaken.

'Tell me, Mr. Utterson,' said he, frowning at his handiwork, 'how far have you progressed in your own investigations? Come, come, do not play the innocent with me; I never knew a lawyer who was not at heart a detective – nor *vice versa*, for that matter.' He raised his eyes from the pipe to those of our visitor. They were piercing. Gone was the languorous figure of a few moments before; he had shed that cocoon and spread his wings to swoop down upon whatever piece of solid evidence he could find which would bear his weight. At such moments the force of his personality was astounding. Utterson fidgeted beneath his fierce scrutiny.

'I can see the futility of attempting to conceal anything from you,' said he, setting down his glass. 'Very well. Yes, I did investigate, for as Henry Jekyll's solicitor I owed him that much, though I feared that you'd accuse me of meddling. I went first to Dr. Hastie Lanyon of Cavendish Square, a mutual friend – I should venture to say that apart from myself he is the oldest friend that Jekyll has. I was, however, surprised to learn that Lanyon and he had not spoken for some ten years, a rift having opened between them over some difference of opinion regarding a scientific subject. Of Edward Hyde he could tell me nothing.'

'One moment,' Holmes interjected. 'Did he not mention the specific difference which created the rift?'

Utterson shook his head. 'He gave no indication, other than to condemn Jekyll's theories as "unscientific balderdash." The very memory of it made him livid with rage.'

'Interesting. But continue.'

'There is little else to relate, save for my meeting with Hyde.'

Holmes paused in the midst of lighting his pipe. 'A meeting, you say? When? Where?'

'It was brief but memorable.' The lawyer shuddered and sipped hastily at his wine. 'That scene and its aftermath are the reason I spent most of today wandering the streets of London, as you were so quick to perceive. I was debating with myself over what should be my next course of action.

'After I left Lanyon, I became convinced that the only way to get to the bottom of this mystery was to force an interview with the principal figure involved. To that end, I set up a vigil at the door which Enfield had pointed out, that which I knew led to the old dissecting-room which Henry Jekyll used for a laboratory, and the only place at which I could reasonably expect to encounter Hyde sooner or later. It was a lonesome occupation, that wait, and I think that I can say with some certainty that it has rid me of any aspirations which I might have entertained towards becoming a detective.

'I fancy that I became a familiar figure to passersby – particularly one young lady of dubious occupation who never tired of attempting to ply her trade with me, no matter how many times I declined the offer. At any rate, it was past ten o'clock on a clear, cold night – last night, if I may put this account into some perspective as regards time – when my patience was finally rewarded and I beheld the object of my attention.

'I heard first his footstep across the street, and I knew immediately that it was he, for I had witnessed all manner of gaits during my days and nights of waiting, and there was not one of them which came close to this odd, springing walk. I drew back into the shadows. No sooner had I done so than this smallish, plainly-dressed creature rounded the corner and strode across the thoroughfare in the direction of the door, fishing inside his trouser pocket as he went. At the door he drew out a key and was about to insert it in the lock when I approached him.

'My hand upon his shoulder startled him. He gripped his cane like a weapon, and, though his face and expression were hidden in shadow beneath the brim of his dull top hat, I had every reason to believe that he intended to use the heavy crook upon me. This was a natural enough reaction, the streets of London being what they are at night; nevertheless, I was glad of my own stick, for he seemed quite capable of carrying out his unspoken threat. I introduced myself hastily and made mention of our mutual acquaintanceship with Henry Jekyll.

'He acknowledged his identity in a strange, repressed guttural, but his face remained in concealment. I asked if he might admit me. He said that that would be unnecessary, as Jekyll was not at home. He then asked how it was that I recognised him. I ignored the question and requested that he show me his face, that I might know him again. There was a moment's hesitation and then, defiantly, he swung about so that the glow of the corner gas lamp fell full upon his countenance.'

He sipped again at his wine, as if the memory had chilled him suddenly. 'It was a face which I do not care to see again, Mr. Holmes. I never met a man whom I so disliked – nay, hated – upon sight alone. It seemed that he was inflicted with some ghastly deformity, and yet if you pressed me I would be helpless to name just what it was about him which was not right. I would be hard put to describe him, yet I would recognise him again in an instant. All I can say is that I was moved to absolute revulsion.'

'If I may say so, those are strange words coming from a lawyer,' observed Holmes, drawing at his pipe.

'Edward Hyde is the sort which inspires strange words,' Utterson returned. 'In spite of my reaction, however, I managed to mutter some inanity to acknowledge the small favour which he had done me in showing himself, to which he replied – quite irrelevantly, I thought – by supplying me with his address in Soho. This caused me no little concern, for I divined from it that he was informing me where he could be reached in the matter of Jekyll's will. It was as if he expected to collect his inheritance at any time. Again he asked me how I knew him; I gave him to believe that Jekyll had described him to me.

'I was unprepared for his reaction. He flew into a rage and accused me of lying. I stammered some sort of defence, but before I could finish he unlocked the door, swept inside, and slammed the door in my face, leaving me standing alone upon the pavement.

'I remained there a moment or two, and then, determined still to plumb the depths of the case, went round the corner and knocked upon Jekyll's door. This section of the building, which fronts upon a busier street, is the more respectable for its well-kept appearance, in sharp contrast with the homely facade of the adjoining block. I was admitted by the butler, Poole, who informed me that his master was out. I mentioned seeing Hyde go in by the old dissecting-room door and asked if he did this often. Poole said that he did, and that Jekyll had left standing instructions for all the servants to obey him. The servants, he added, see little of the fellow save when they meet by chance in the rear of the house; it seems that Hyde is not in the habit of dining there, nor of remaining long when he visits. And those, Mr. Holmes, are the facts as far as I have been able to gather them.'

'Admirable!' exclaimed the other, who was standing with his back to the fire, smoking his pipe. 'It's a pity you opted for the legal profession, Mr. Utterson. Scotland Yard is in sore need of energetic fathomers such as yourself. You have made my task much simpler by sparing me the trouble of collecting the information which you have supplied.'

'You are interested, then?' Utterson rose.

'The case presents a number of intriguing particulars,' Holmes acknowledged. 'One final question. In all the years during which you have known Dr. Jekyll, have you ever known him to be guilty of a serious indiscretion?'

'I know what you are driving at,' said the other, 'but I fear that my answer will disappoint you. As long as I have been Henry Jekyll's confidant, his actions, to my knowledge, have never been anything less than those of a gentleman. Of course, I did not know him during his student days at the University of Edinburgh and can tell you nothing about his conduct then. I doubt, however, that he could have been guilty of any malfeasance serious enough to embarrass him after all of these years. He is and has always been a credit to his calling.'

'What of his relationship with women?'

The lawyer smiled faintly beneath his moustache. 'Henry Jekyll and I are confirmed bachelors.'

'These are deep waters indeed,' reflected the detective, fingering his pipe.

'Tell me, Mr. Holmes; is it blackmail?'

'I think that it is very probable.'

'Well, I care for my friend and, dark secret or no, I do not intend to see him suffer any further humiliation at the hands of a man whom upon the evidence I can only consider a fiend. But before I can free him I must know the nature of that secret, and that is why I am here. Will you accept the case?'

Holmes stepped away from the mantelpiece, turning so as to avoid meeting my warning gaze. 'I can think of nothing that I'd like better than to turn whatever feeble skills I may possess towards the clearing up of this problem.'

'One caution,' Utterson said. 'It is imperative that Jekyll never know of your interest in the matter.'

'You have my word that as long as it is in my power to keep him in the dark he will remain so.'

The two clasped hands, and after Holmes had secured the addresses of Jekyll, Utterson, and Hyde as the last had been given the lawyer and scribbled them on his shirt cuff, he bade our visitor farewell, sending him off with words of encouragement and a promise to keep him informed. Once he had gone, my companion turned to me.

'What does your Medical Directory have to say upon the subject of Dr. Henry Jekyll, Watson?' he asked.

I swallowed my anger with him for the time being and took down the requested volume from among the books upon my shelf. I flipped through the pages, found the passage I was looking for, and read:

Jekyll, Henry William, M.D., D.C.L., LL.D., F.R.S., 1856, London. Lecturer, from 1871 to 1874, at the University of London. Developer of the Jekyll tranquiliser for violent mental cases. Worked with Porter Thaler, M.D.,

B.A., M.A., M.R.C.S., during the latter's experiments in chemotherapy for the criminally insane. Noted for his ongoing researches into the causes and cures of mental disease. Author of 'Law and the Dual Personality,' Lancet, 1876. 'The Legality of Insanity,' Journal of Psychology, August 1880. 'The War Between the Members,' British Medical Journal, February 1882. Declined the offer of a knighthood in 1881 and again in 1882.

'"The War Between the Members",' Holmes mused. 'An intriguing title. I should be interested in reading the article which goes with it.'

'I came across it quite recently whilst going through my back numbers,' said I, trading the big Directory for the slimmer *British Medical Journal* for February of the previous year. 'The editors gave no little space to a rather outlandish theory of his regarding – here, I've found it. "The War Between the Members," by Henry Jekyll, M.D. D.C.L., LL.D., and so forth. Shall I read some of it?'

'Please do.'

'"When a great man dies",' I read, '"we are given to discourse upon the nature of the man, and to list the glowing achievements which this nature produced during his span. What we ignore – and 'ignore' is the proper word, since we all know that it exists but prefer not to speak of it – is his second nature, that baser, less noble member which, depending upon the degree to which it is suppressed, threatens to drag its owner down meaner channels than those its lofty counterpart has chosen. For man is not one but two, and those two are for ever in conflict over which shall be the master. It is the victor which decides what direction the man's life will take." It goes on in that vein for six pages.' I closed the book.

'Eloquent,' said Holmes.

'But simplistic. He says nothing that everyone does not already know.'

'Which is, perhaps, why it is important to say it. But I wonder that it appeared in a medical journal. It smacks of philosophy rather than science.'

'He makes the point later on that understanding the conflict between man's two selves may one day lead to a cure for diseases of the mind. Far-fetched, I call it.'

But Holmes was not listening. He thrust a hand inside the pocket of his frock-coat and stared at the smoke floating from his pipe towards the ceiling. 'Two natures, one noble, the other base. I wonder if it is perhaps Jekyll's own baser nature which made him a target. If he is indeed a target. A most tantalising problem, this.'

'I trust that the solution is worth the danger to your health,' I remonstrated, for I could control my fury no longer. 'It is obvious that I failed in my attempts to make you appreciate the importance of this holiday.'

'Holiday be damned!' he cried unexpectedly. 'Blackmailers are the absolute worst of criminals, for they bleed their victims dry and leave nothing but the empty husk behind. There is, for instance, a man in Hampstead – with whom there will one day be a reckoning – who holds the fates of a dozen men and women in his hands, and who dallies with them as does a child with his cup and ball. No, Watson, there will be no holiday whilst one of our worthiest citizens squirms beneath the thumb of such a scoundrel. Nottingham is postponed, and we shall speak no more of it until we have closed the book upon the strange case of Dr. Jekyll and Mr. Hyde.' He snatched his great-coat and hat from their hook and put them on.

'Where are we bound?' I asked.

'It's going to be a fine night, Watson,' said he, handing me my own outer garments. 'What say you to a little journey down to Soho?'

Three

Q

A CONFRONTATION IN SOHO

A few minutes' travel by hansom saw us in Soho Square, that haphazard conglomeration of dingy streets and ramshackle buildings in which a dozen different nationalities flourish like so many varieties of exotic plants in a hothouse. It was a clear night, and yet the scenery was scarcely discernible in the inadequate light trickling through the sooty panes of the gas lamps which stood on every corner. Some vandal had hurled a paving-stone through the one nearest the address which we sought, extinguishing it, so that our driver had to climb down from his seat and strike a match beneath the wrought-iron numbers upon the door before he could be certain that he had brought us to the right place.

'This is it, gentlemen,' he announced cheerily, shaking out the match as he returned to the hansom. 'Though why a pair of upstandin' gentlemen like yourselves'd be visitin' the kind of bloke what lives in a dump like this is beyond me, if you don't mind me sayin' so.'

Ignoring the implied question, Holmes alighted and handed the driver a half-crown. 'There's more where that came from if you'll take your cab round the corner and wait for us,' the detective told him.

'Blimey!' exclaimed the other, secreting the coin in his coat pocket. 'For 'arf a crown I'd kidnap the Tsar of Rooshia single-handed.'

'That won't be necessary. Just wait round the corner.' When he had clattered off: 'It's a rare fellow who speaks his mind like that, Watson. He'd sing a different tune if he knew what the man who resides in this particular "dump" is heir to. Did you think to bring your revolver, by the way?'

'I did not think it necessary.'

'A pity. Well, we have our sticks.' He placed his hand upon my arm. 'Do not be alarmed, old fellow; I expect no trouble of the physical sort. But one cannot be too careful after what we have heard concerning this man Hyde.' So saying, he led the way to the low wooden door of the squat, two-storey dwelling and rapped upon the panel.

The door was opened by an old woman wearing a severe black dress with a collar of white lace, in the center of which reposed a plain ivory brooch which she twisted between the fingers of one hand whilst studying the two men on her stoop. Once the ensemble had been very fine, but in the intervening years the black had begun to turn purple, the white had yellowed, and the ivory had grown loose in its setting of tarnished silver. The face above the frayed collar was of a hue and texture reminiscent of that same ivory, and this together with the pure silver of her hair, might have made her a genteel figure but for the avaricious gleam in her eye and an expression which denoted pure hypocrisy. Swiftly placing her role in the household, I was suddenly grateful for a landlady like Mrs. Hudson. I would hardly have trusted such a creature as this with a key to my rooms.

'If it's lodgings you're after,' she said, looking from one to the other of us, 'I've rooms upstairs in back. Rates are five quid per week in advance, and I shan't sit still for tobacco nor dogs.'

'My dear woman, we are not after lodgings but have come on a visit,' said Holmes. 'You have, I believe, a tenant by the name of Edward Hyde; it is he whom we wish to see.'

At the mention of the name, she drew back from the doorway as if Holmes had produced a snake. 'You are friends of his?' Nervously she twisted the brooch, straining the material to which it was pinned.

'I fail to see what difference that makes,' he responded.

'He is from home. He is often thus sometimes for weeks at a stretch. I have not seen him for some days. Come back later in the week.' She started to close the door. Holmes blocked it with his foot.

'May we at least see his rooms?'

Outrage at his action and strange request dawned over the old woman's features, but the expression quickly changed to one of greed as Holmes held a glittering sovereign before her face. She started to reach for it, then her hand drew back and resumed fiddling with the brooch.

'I cannot allow you to do that,' said she. 'The gentleman would be very angry.'

She said it calmly enough, but fear was stamped upon her every feature. The hatred and terror which she felt for her lodger were nearly tangible. What sort of monster was this Edward Hyde?

Holmes made his voice gruff. 'Very well, if that's the way you prefer it. We can always get a warrant. Come along, Inspector.' He turned away. She caught his sleeve.

'Why didn't you say that you were with the police?' She flung the door wide. Holmes winked at me surreptitiously and led the way inside.

The door shut, the woman wiped her hands absentmindedly upon her apron, staring at the coin in Holmes's hand. 'I am a poor woman, sir,' she ventured.

He gave her the sovereign. 'Your silence is of course included in the price.'

She cackled mirthlessly and dropped the coin into the pocket of her apron. 'You needn't pay for that, sir. Hyde would kill me if he found out. He is in trouble, then?' Her expression became eager. When Holmes did not reply, she shrugged her shoulders, seized a lamp and a ring of keys from a table beside the door, and, picking up her skirts, led us across a faded rug and up a narrow and exceedingly noisy staircase.

'What sort of tenant is Hyde?' asked the detective on the way up.

'He is quiet and he pays his rent on time. That is good enough for me.'

'Yet he does not seem to have made himself popular.'

'No other lodgers will live beneath the same roof.'

'Indeed! And why is that?'

'If you had ever met him, you would not ask that question.'

Stopping at the first door in the hallway atop the stairs, she unlocked it and pushed it open. 'There they are, sir; two rooms only. I beg you to do whatever it is you have to do quickly, and leave everything as you found it.' She handed Holmes the lamp and descended.

'Is it not unlawful to impersonate a police officer?' I asked Holmes once she was out of earshot.

'I did not say that we were police officers. If she leapt to that conclusion, who am I to contradict her?' He turned his attention to the open doorway. 'Come, Watson.'

Somewhat surprisingly, the two rooms occupied by Hyde, in contrast to the rest of the house, were spacious and decorated in the finest taste, with a rich carpet upon the floor of the combination bed-and-sitting-room, heavy velvet curtains over the single window, an exquisite oil upon one wall, and in the bathroom a silver basin upon a marble stand. There was, in addition, a closet stocked with expensive wines, a bureau, a pedestal table, two armchairs, and a tall wardrobe beside the bed in which hung half a dozen suits of varying degrees of richness, from coarsest wool to the very best that New Bond Street had to offer. One hanger was empty.

'His dress-suit, I fancy,' said Holmes, fingering the last item. 'I see none here, and yet he seems to own every other form of attire required of a gentleman in this over-dressed age. Wherever he is staying, I should wager that it is not far removed from society.'

'Judging by what I've heard of the man, I would hardly call him a gentleman,' said I.

'Quite right, Watson. These days, however, gentlemanly status seems to be more a question of appearance than conduct. I sometimes think that a gorilla would pass without comment at one of our West End social functions, so long as his shirt front remains spotless and he holds his teacup in the proper fashion.'

'He seems well off, at any rate.'

'And why not? His benefactor is one of the wealthiest men in London. But we are not here to confirm his credit.'

Several pairs of boots reposed side by side at the bottom of the wardrobe. Holmes examined these briefly, then replaced them and closed the door. After that his search began in earnest. I stood back out of the way as he slid open the drawers of the bureau, starting with the one on top, and, carefully so as to avoid dislodging anything, groped among the contents for I knew not what. Whilst searching through the second drawer, he uttered an exclamation of satisfaction and drew out a rectangular grey object which I recognised as an account book, its cover inscribed with the name of one of our oldest and most respected banking institutions. He opened it, whistled once whilst running his finger down the column of figures which he found inside, then closed it and returned it to its former place without further comment. After going through the rest of the drawers, he turned his attention to the remainder of the room.

He overlooked nothing, not even the trash basket in the corner, the contents of which he sorted through with both hands as he knelt beside it. He felt beneath the windowsill and peeped under the bed. At length he produced his pocket lens and crawled along the edge of the carpet, peering at it through the thick glass. Finally he stood up and returned the instrument to his pocket.

'What —' I began to ask. Holmes placed a finger to his lips.

He turned and, with a sly expression, crossed the room upon cat's feet to the door. There he paused dramatically with his hand upon the knob, then suddenly twisted it and yanked open the door.

The old landlady spilled into the room amidst a rustle of skirts and fell sprawling to the floor.

'The next time you seek to listen at the keyhole,' Holmes informed her, smiling, 'I would suggest that you climb the staircase upon the very edge of the steps, where they are not apt to creak quite so loudly. And lift your skirts as you near the door; your approach put me in mind of closing-time at a silk merchant's.' He extended a hand to help her to her feet.

The woman said, 'Well!' got up, dusted herself off, and turned to go.

'One moment,' said Holmes.

She paused and glared at him, her face a mask of suspicion and indignation.

'What can you tell us of your lodger's movements during the hours of daylight?'

Her expression grew stubborn. Holmes sighed and handed her another coin. She polished it upon her apron and pocketed it. It clinked against the one he had given her earlier.

'He has none,' said she. 'The few times that he has been here in the daytime were spent in his rooms. He seldom ventures out before dark and does not return until almost dawn.'

'Does he work nights?'

She cackled maliciously. 'Not unless his work calls for him to sit all night drinking and carousing in a pub. I have seen him in Stunner's on the corner when I go there for my dollop of rum. I have this condition, you see.' She placed a hand to her throat and coughed delicately.

'Thank you. That is all.'

Holmes took down the lamp where he had left it atop the bureau and we quitted the room, the landlady turning to lock the door behind us. At the foot of the staircase he handed her the lamp, wished her goodnight, and together we stepped out into the crisp air of the street.

'There is the corner and that, I believe, is Stunner's,' the detective observed, pointing out the neglected facade of a public-house two doors down. 'Would you object to a bracer of whiskey-and-soda before we return to Baker Street?'

I said that I would not, and we struck off in that direction.

'Are you not going to tell me what you learnt?' I asked impatiently after we had gone half a dozen steps in silence.

He rubbed his hands together. 'Just enough to make me wish for more. I know, for instance, that Hyde has no source of income aside from his famous friend's largesse, and that he has been something less than frugal where those gains are concerned. Moreover, his taste in women runs towards the lowest classes of society and is on a par only with his preference in entertainment, both of which are considerably meaner than his over-all standard of living, which is princely. On a more physical level, he is five feet, one inch in height, is slightly pigeon-toed, and smokes Cavendish tobacco. Everything else about him remains a mystery.'

This astonishing compendium of facts, gleaned from so brief an examination of Hyde's effects, filled me with curiosity, but before I could question my companion upon how he had reached his conclusions we had stepped across the threshold into the public-house and the time had come to hold my tongue.

What struck me first about the establishment was the conviction that the owner was trying to save money on gas. So few of the fixtures were lit that, until my eyes grew accustomed to the gloom, I literally had difficulty in distinguishing my hand before my face. Even then I was forced to rely upon Holmes's unique ability to see in the dark in order to reach the bar by allowing him to lead me by the arm between the tables and chairs. It was a large, low-ceilinged room, redolent of the usual ale and sawdust, and crowded to capacity even at that early hour. The atmosphere was a confusion of voices chattering in many different tongues, some raised in jollification, others edged with anger, still others sunken into the monotonous rumble of utter boredom. Behind the bar a solid block of a man with great swinging jowls and a head of thick dark hair which seemed to grow straight up from his brows with no forehead in between broke off his conversation with an inebriate who was slumped across from him and turned to face us as we approached.

'What'll it be, mates?' Despite his approximation of East End slang, it was obvious from his ponderous accent that the man was German.

'I should like a whisky-and-soda, and my friend will have the same,' said Holmes. When the drinks were poured: 'I do not see my other friend around this evening, and yet I am given to understand that he frequents this establishment. Has Edward Hyde been in of late?'

A look of absolute loathing twisted the German's heavy features into a grotesque caricature. He seized a not-too-clean rag from beneath the bar and proceeded to polish the marred top with savage movements of his huge right hand. 'Not lately, mates,' he growled. 'And if you're friends of his, I suggest that you drink up and get out. I'll brook no trouble in my place of business.'

Holmes raised his eyebrows. 'He has been troublesome?'

'You see that mirror?' Stürmer — if that was his name — jerked a thumb over his shoulder in the direction of a cracked mirror behind the bar, over which was pasted a sign reading NO CREDIT. 'Last time he was in there was the devil of a row, and before I could put a stop to it some bloke chucked a full mug of beer at Hyde, he ducked, and there's the result. I threw the lot of them out and said that if I ever saw any of them in here again I'd bend my billiard-cue over their skulls.'

'Did Hyde start it?'

'Well, not so's you could blame him for it. Some little French clerk with a bag on took one look at him and called him a name I wouldn't care to repeat to my mother in Hamburg. Hyde snarled something back — I didn't hear it, he has this whispery growl — and that's when the trouble started. He's bad news, that one is. I'm glad to be rid of him.'

Holmes thanked him and paid for our drinks. At his suggestion, we picked up our glasses and left the bar for a table in the corner which had just been vacated by a pair of drunken slatterns.

'Upon the face of it,' said Holmes after we had sat down, 'it would be a capital mistake for Hyde to make a bid for public office. He is not famous for his popularity.'

'I am burning with curiosity,' said I. 'You and I saw the same things in Hyde's rooms a little while ago, and yet I admit that I was unable to determine even a small part of the things which you learnt about him.'

He smiled and sipped at his drink. 'Of course you were. You are a man of more than a few talents, Watson, but observation and deduction do not number among them. And yet the clues were there, if you knew what to look for.'

'Then perhaps you will explain how you divined that Hyde has no income apart from that provided by Jekyll, and that he has not been frugal with it.'

'I take no pride in that conclusion, for it was a surface matter, with very little deduction involved. You will remember that I found his account-book.'

'You whistled once whilst reading it.'

'I had every reason to react in that fashion. His balance is far from small, and the records show that he has made substantial deposits at irregular intervals. That they were substantial, and that the entries were irregular, precludes the probability of their being wages, which are seldom so large and are paid out regularly. From what the landlady told us of his movements, it is unlikely that he is gainfully employed. That the deposits were the results of investments is also unlikely, since the sums were in round figures, with no odd pounds, shillings, or pence left over. Gifts of money are usually made in round figures. Further, since all of the sums were similar, I decided that they were the gift of one person. I confess that my choice of Jekyll as the giver is pure surmise, but under the circumstances he seems the most likely candidate.'

'And his lack of frugality?'

'His preference in dress is costly, which I admit is hardly a sign of reckless spending; but when I go through a man's trash basket and find that he has thrown away two perfectly good, though soiled, silk shirts rather than take the trouble of having them laundered, I am tempted to think him something of a spendthrift.'

'Well, that seems simple enough. But what of his taste in women and entertainment, and his princely standard of living?'

'As for women, the cast-off shirts which I mentioned were smudged with two different shades of rouge, both of which can be had in any of the shabbier women's shops near the waterfront. I have made study of the many different types of cosmetics used by the fair sex, and toy with the idea of someday producing a monograph upon the subject. His choice of entertainment I judged mean as well after finding in the basket no fewer than nine ticket-stubs from one of more our *risqué* music-halls off

Buck's Row. A man who would return eight times must like what he sees. Turning to his standard of living, that is evident in his casual treatment of his wardrobe – the shirts again – and in the many withdrawals which he has made from his banking-account to finance his way of life.'

'That leaves his height, the fact that he is pigeon-toed, and the tobacco he smokes.'

He smiled. 'Come now, Watson. Surely you saw that only a man who fits the dimensions I quoted would be comfortable in clothes the size of Hyde's, and you could not have failed to note that the soles of his boots were worn more on the outside edges of the toes than anywhere else, indicating an inward twist.'

I flushed in my embarrassment. 'I did not, but I should have. And his tobacco?'

'Cavendish, or my monograph upon the distinction between the various tobaccos based upon their ashes was written in vain. The greenish-grey traces which I found upon the edge of the carpet could belong to no other. But what, in the name of the devil!'

The cause of this ejaculation was the dramatic entrance of a singular figure into the public-house: a minuscule, almost dwarfish man dressed in evening clothes, complete with shining top hat and a scarlet-lined opera cape which flowed behind him as he burst through the door and settled about his heels as he stood in the middle of the room, gripping his cane in one hand and casting savage glances into every corner. His head was large, his face lean and wolfish, marked by flaring nostrils and a pair of eyebrows which soared upwards from the bridge of his nose like bat's-wings, to disappear into the shadows beneath the brim of his hat. Aside from those points, it was an unremarkable face, save for the fact that I hated it upon sight.

I like to think that I am a man who does not allow himself to be carried away by his emotions, and yet it shames me to admit that, just as the sorrowful countenance of G. J. Utterson had won my sympathy before he had even stated his problem, the appearance of this stranger aroused a hatred in me such as I had not felt since a bullet from a Ghazi rifle had nearly taken my life at the Battle of Mai-wand three years before. It was a primitive emotion, having no basis in reason, and because of that it was unshakeable.

'Where are the felons?' he roared.

For all of its volume, his voice remained a harsh, insinuating whisper, like a file rasping against rusted steel. Every eye in the place was upon him. His murderous gaze swept the room, finally falling upon Holmes and me, whereupon it took on an even more dangerous glint.

'There they are, the cursed scoundrels!'

In two leaps he was at our table. For a tense moment he stood looking from one to the other of us, his breath passing sibilantly through his arched nostrils. 'Which of you is the ringleader?' he demanded.

'You, I take it, are Edward Hyde,' said Holmes, rising. He towered over the new-comer by nearly a foot.

'Ah, so you are the one behind it!' The small man took a cautious step backwards, balancing his cane in one hand like a bludgeon. He had short hands, muscular and covered with hair; I was reminded, if I may bring forth yet another beast for comparison, of the paws of an ape. 'You and your companion entered my rooms tonight without my permission, and do not attempt to deny it. I smelt the burnt oil of the lamp you used. When I confronted my landlady with the knowledge, she broke down and told me everything. She described you both in detail and said that you walked off in this direction.'

'I am Sherlock Holmes, and this is my friend and colleague, Dr. John H. Watson. We have long been eager to make your acquaintance, Mr. Hyde. Would you care to join us in a whisky-and-soda whilst we discuss this like gentlemen?'

'Gentlemen? You are common burglars! Sir, I demand satisfaction!' he raised his cane.

I leapt to my feet, prepared to come to my friend's defence. He shook his head and waved me back.

'Thank you, Watson, but this is my affair.' He assumed a boxer's stance.

For a charged moment it appeared that the two might actually come to blows; there was a scraping of chairs as the customers seated near us vacated their tables, and Holmes and Hyde squared off beside our own in the manner of warring rams. But before either of them could make a move Stürmer came striding out from behind the bar bearing a two-foot length of loaded billiard-cue and brought it smashing down onto the table between them with a report like an explosion. The noise made both of them jump.

'I said no rows and, by God, I meant it!' The German's booming voice set every glass in the room to rattling. He caught my eye. 'Take your friend and go. I'll hold back Hyde till you're out of sight. After that, whatever happens don't concern me. *Schnell!*'

Holmes and I needed no further invitation. We picked up our hats and sticks from the table and headed for the door whilst Stürmer held a fuming Hyde at bay with his club.

'You see the value of foresight, old fellow,' said Holmes as we stepped into the hansom waiting around the corner. 'When one sets out to commit a criminal act, an escape well planned is its own reward.'

It was his last attempt to place a light face upon the night's activities. On the way home the detective sank into a deeply brooding frame of mind. 'Dark forces at work here, Watson,' said he, staring out into the gloom that closed in upon the cab.

I made no reply, for I was seeking to duplicate the methods of my friend in analysing my strangely primitive reaction to the character of

Edward Hyde. The threats which he had uttered were quite beside the point, since I had formed my opinion before I was even aware of his identity, or of whom his anger was directed against. Try as I might, however, I succeeded only in recalling the following nursery-rhyme from my childhood, which until that evening had always seemed the merest bit of nonsense, but which had now taken on a most profound meaning:

I do not love thee, Dr. Fell,
The reason why I cannot tell;
But this I know and know full well,
I do not love thee, Dr. Fell.

Four

BLANK WALLS AND WALNUT-STAIN

W e won't starve to death, at any rate,' announced my companion, once we had returned to our digs and the gas was lit. 'Mrs. Hudson is a treasure among land-ladies.'

The source of his praise was a cold fowl supper which had been laid out upon the sideboard in our absence. We sat down over it and two glasses of Beaune – it had been no evening for the gentler influence of port – and ate for some minutes in silence. Then: 'What now?' I asked.

'Sleep,' said he. 'We shall need all we can get, for tomorrow will prove a busy day for both of us. You, for instance – if my advice is worth anything – are going to pay a call upon your club and renew old acquaintanceships. It has been far too long since your last visit.'

'And you?'

'I shall be doing my level best to keep the cabmen of this city in business as I travel from bank to records bureau to Scotland Yard and points beyond in an attempt to ferret out the life story of Edward Hyde, celebrated *dilettante* and heir to the Jekyll fortune. "Know thine enemy", Watson, for an enemy is what he is most certainly shaping up to be.'

'Your health –' said I.

'– will be none the worse for a brisk jaunt about London,' he finished. 'You are always after me to take exercise.'

'So long as you do not over-do it.'

'My dear fellow, it is inactivity which exhausts me.' He got up from the table. 'Into the arms of Morpheus, then, and when next we speak it is my hope that we shall have a solid foundation of data upon which we can build some sturdy conclusions.'

But I was not taken in by his sudden desire for sleep. Long after I retired, as I lay awake sorting through the vagaries in the relationship of Dr. Jekyll and Mr. Hyde, I smelt tobacco-smoke and heard the steady tread of Holmes's feet as he paced to and fro in the bedroom below mine, drawing on his pipe and mulling over the problem upon an intellectual plane which was without doubt far loftier than my own. Such late hours were dangerous to his constitution, but I was in no mood to hear another lecture upon the evils of extortion *versus* the well-being of a single mortal. I went to sleep with that monotonous tramping still in my ears.

Holmes had breakfasted and gone by the time I arose the next morning; there was a note upon the sideboard reminding me of his advice of the night before, but since it was raining heavily outside I decided to forgo my club and settled down instead to a day of reading. It was close upon five o'clock when the door opened and in dragged my friend with a crestfallen look upon his face. He nodded a halfhearted greeting and slumped heavily into his velvet-lined armchair.

'You have just come from the Bank of England, I perceive,' said I, hiding what I fear was an impish smile behind the book I was reading.

He glanced at me in some surprise. At length he smiled, in spite of his obvious exhaustion. 'Wherever did you obtain that information?' he asked.

I reveled in his reaction. It was not often that I was able to impress him, and it gave me added pleasure to know that for once I had bested him at his own game.

'Elementary,' I declared, closing my book and laying it aside. 'You mentioned last night that one of the places you were planning to visit was a bank. When last I passed the Bank of England they were tearing up the street in front of the establishment, revealing a distinctive murky red clay beneath the pavement – a sample of which adheres to the sole of your left boot. You did not walk around it, hence your business was in the bank itself.'

Whilst I spoke, the detective had been examining the sole in question. Now he returned it to the floor and smacked his knee gleefully with the palm of his hand.

'Excellent! Really, Watson, sounding your depths is a frustrating experience; I seem never to strike bottom. Your talents of observation have always been admirable, but now you have learnt to apply them practically. I congratulate you upon your growth.'

'Then I was correct? You visited the Bank of England?'

'No, I was nowhere near the institution.'

I stared. 'But the clay – !'

'Not clay, paint. They were touching up the sign over the entrance to Bradley's when I stopped in for some shag, and I had the misfortune to step into the drippings. But do not be glum, old fellow; you have provided the one bright spot in an otherwise bleak day.'

I nodded, for that had been my intention, though not quite in that manner.

'Your investigations failed, then?'

'On the contrary, they proved most bountiful, up to a point.' He produced a pouch and began filling his cherry-wood.

'And beyond that?'

'Nothing. The bank I went to was the one in which Hyde keeps his account, which you would have deduced had you not fallen into the common trap of allowing a clue to obscure your own memory. The cashier whom I interviewed was reluctant to answer my questions until I convinced him that I had entered into a business dealing with Hyde and was confirming his credit, after which he became positively garrulous. It seems that Hyde opened the account a year ago. He had kept none previously.'

'That does not seem so very unusual.'

'Hear me out. From there I went to the records office in Whitehall, where a search of three and one half hours failed to turn up the name of Edward Hyde upon any document. Whoever he is, he was not born in England, nor does he own any property here under that name. The files at Scotland Yard proved equally empty. That left but one other place to try, and you can image my reluctance to go there after our experience of last night. Fortunately, our quarry was out again today, but it cost me no small sum to obtain the information which I required from his landlady. She is a very frightened woman today, Watson; I fear that her boarder has presented her with a grim ultimatum where any further doings with me are concerned. Thank heaven for our gracious Queen's image in gold, which seems to outweigh such arguments.

'It seems that Hyde took up residence at the Soho address at about the time he opened the afore-mentioned banking-account, and that in lieu of references from his last landlord he tendered six weeks' rent in advance. He has, of course, said nothing to her about his former life.' He shook his head and ignited his pipe. 'It is most maddening. From whatever angle one approaches the problem, he encounters a blank wall *circa* October of 1882. It is as if Edward Hyde simply did not exist before that date.

'Perhaps "Edward Hyde" is a pseudonym,' I ventured.

'Very likely, but what good does that do us, unless we have his real name as well? I described him in some detail for the detectives with whom I spoke at the Yard; it brought forth no flood of memories.'

'He is not the kind one forgets easily.' I shuddered at the recollection of last night's encounter.

Holmes nodded and sent a great blue wreath of smoke floating ceilingwards. 'He is rather odious, is he not? I don't think that I have ever met a man upon whose countenance evil is more clearly stamped, and I have travelled among London's worst. But this is getting us nowhere.' He got up and strode towards his bedroom.

'Where are you going?' I rose.

'Where you need not follow,' said he, over his shoulder. The door closed behind him.

So sharp had been his retort, and so unexpected, that for a moment I was struck speechless and made no reply. As I thought about it, however, I was glad that I had not, for it was obvious from Holmes's manner that he was operating beneath a severe strain. The activity of the past two days had placed a greater burden upon his weakened constitution than even I had realised. Seized with a sudden fear, I glanced towards the mantelpiece, but was relieved to see that his cocaine bottle and the morocco case in which he kept his hypodermic syringe were still there. His health was in a dangerous enough state without the added influence of those drug habits about which I have written elsewhere in these chronicles. I decided then that his bedroom was the best place for him at this point, and so did not pursue the matter, but lit a cigarette and sat down to consider the problem upon which we were engaged. This of course was useless, and all I gained was a sore throat. I was tossing a third cigarette-end into the grate when the bedroom door opened and a surprising figure stepped into the room.

In appearance it was a Lascar, one of those native sailors who ply their trade upon the East Indian seas. Beneath a crimson head-scarf, a lean face as swarthy as tree-bark stared with its one good eye cocked towards me, the other hidden behind a greasy black patch; from beneath the patch a hideous whitish scar described a ragged semi-circle down his left cheek to the corner of a sullen mouth. From the corner protruded the stub of a thick black cigar, now extinguished. His clothes were coarse and smeared all over with tar, his boots canvas and worn through at the toes. Had I not known that Holmes had been alone in the chamber, and that there was no way into it save through the door through which he had passed earlier, I would have been at a loss to identify the wretch who stood before me. From head to toe, it was not the sort of person whom I would prefer to have at my back in an East End alley.

'Holmes,' said I, 'this time you have really out-done yourself. I should be surprised if you are not arrested the moment you step outdoors looking like that.'

He chuckled. 'Thank you, Watson. I can always count upon you for an honest appraisal. You do not think that it is over-done?'

'That depends upon your destination. I would not recommend, for instance, that you attend the theatre in that condition.'

'And yet that is precisely where I am headed.'

'My dear Holmes!'

Again he chuckled. 'Calm yourself, Watson. In the crowd which frequents this particular establishment I shall be quite inconspicuous, I assure you. You will, I am certain, recall those ticket-stubs which I mentioned having found in Hyde's rooms; it is that theatre which I plan to attend.'

'May I ask why?'

'His landlady, demonstrating a practical nature for which I should scarcely have credited her, told me that she had found a ticket for tonight's performance in the pocket of his coat before sending it out to be cleaned this morning. My chances of finding him there this evening, then, appear better than even.'

'What do you hope to learn by that?'

He shrugged. 'Who can say? Perhaps nothing. Perhaps everything. In any case, I shall learn more by a close observation of his habits than by wasting time with bureaucratic channels. No, no, my dear fellow, keep your seat; I shan't be needing you tonight.'

'You may not need me, but you shall have me nonetheless.' I rose. 'I am aware of the futility of attempting to dissuade you from the course which you have chosen, so I will not do so. However, I do insist that I accompany you to see that you do not over-exert yourself in this affair. Do not argue, Holmes; I defer to your superior knowledge in matters of detection, but when it comes to your health I recognise no master but myself.'

I expected anger, even scorn, but instead he favoured me with a sincere smile and his hand upon my shoulder. 'Dear friend,' he said warmly, 'I did not realise that you felt so strongly about the state of my health. Of course I will not argue with you. You are well rested, I gather, since the dry-ness of your coat yonder and the depletion of this morning's ample coal supply indicates that you disregarded my advice and stayed in today. Tell me, have you ever in your life performed a role upon the stage?'

I had not been prepared for this swift change of subject; it took me a moment to respond. Finally I said: 'I portrayed an oak in my fifth-form production of *A Midsummer Night's Dream!*'

He appeared puzzled. 'No oak has a speaking role in *A Midsummer Night's Dream!*' said he.

'Yes, I know.'

He laughed. 'Well then, you shall not be called upon to speak tonight either. Come along.'

Holmes led me into his bedroom, where a basin filled with some dark liquid stood upon his wash-stand next to the bed. The bed itself, I noticed, was cluttered with unidentifiable paraphernalia. At his direction I took a seat upon the edge of the mattress, whereupon he instructed me to remove my collar and to bathe my hands and face in the liquid. I obeyed, and when I had finished he dipped in his own hands and completed the job round my ears and upon the back of my neck, rubbing with quick, nervous fingers. Next he bent over me, and, picking up various articles from the bed, began to apply things to my face, scraping, shaping, massaging, brushing – for half an hour he proceeded in this fashion until, with a ceremonious flourish, he tossed his instruments back upon the bed, dusted off his palms and stood back.

'Done and done,' said he. 'There is a mirror upon that bureau; perhaps you would care to take a look at yourself before we proceed to the final stage in the transformation of John H. Watson, M.D.'

I did so, and was astounded by what I saw. There, glaring out at me from the depths of the mirror, was a half-caste Oriental of a particularly wicked type. Long, narrow eyes glittered malevolently against a background of yellow-brown skin, on either side of a shapeless lump of nose which looked as if it had been smashed in more than one waterfront brawl; beneath it, a row of opium-stained teeth flashed behind a lank black moustache. From my hairline down, the metamorphosis was complete. I was struck by the realism of this grotesque mask, which could not have been more alien to the face which I was accustomed to shaving each morning. As in so many things, when it came to the art of disguise Holmes was indeed a wizard.

I told him as much. He waved away the compliment. 'You praise me now,' said he, 'but your words may sour later, when you attempt to remove that walnut stain. But try these on; I think that they will harmonise quite smoothly with your new image.'

He had thrown open his trunk and from its recesses drawn out sandals, a filthy pea-jacket, cotton trousers, and a battered bowler, all of which I quickly donned. After that, a final glance towards the mirror was enough to assure me that my mother, were she still living, would not have recognised me.

'Bear in mind that you are now a deaf-mute and that if there is any speaking to be done it is I who shall do it,' Holmes admonished. 'And slip your revolver into your coat pocket, just in case.'

I did so and was about to leave when the detective told me to hold out my hands and, when I obeyed, dumped a double handful of pennies and half-pennies into them.

'What are these for?' I asked.

Amusement sparkled in his single exposed eye. 'To toss at the girls, Watson. To toss at the girls.'

That bore explaining, but as he was already at the door, I decided to abandon it for now, dumped the coins into my trouser pockets, and followed him.

Five

THE HAUNTS OF HYDE

I dare say that we gave Mrs. Hudson something of a turn on our way out, but as she was a most long-suffering woman she accepted Holmes's sketchy explanation for our appearance without protest, and we were allowed to leave through the side door. Transportation was our next difficulty; three times Holmes attempted to hail a cab, and three times he was nearly run down for his efforts as the drivers, exhibiting keen senses of personal danger, whipped up their horses to prevent us from boarding. On the fourth try he found one who was not so particular, and though Holmes had to show him gold in advance, he agreed to convey us to our destination.

Soho was respectable in comparison to the appalling conditions along Buck's Row, where brothels and slaughterhouses were crowded together along filthy streets so narrow that there was hardly room for two carriages to pass without scraping their wheels, and every doorway was occupied by either inebriates or, to use Utterson's quaint phrase, 'women of dubious occupation'. Gas lamps were few and far between, as indeed were policemen; for these reasons, it was no wonder that, once our driver had let us off at the address which Holmes had given him and been paid, he produced his whip and slapped his horse into a brisk trot to quit the area as rapidly as possible.

The building before which we found ourselves was a half century old at least, its soot-darkened façade beginning to crumble and the windows in the upper storeys long since boarded up. Over the entrance, appended by chains to a trusted wrought-iron post, swung a wooden sign upon which the legend THE RED GOOSE could just be made out in letters of faded scarlet. From inside floated the tinkling strains of an out-of-tune piano, punctuated at intervals by peals of drunken laughter.

'We're late, Watson,' Holmes murmured. 'The curtain has gone up.'

The performance had indeed started. A line of scantily-clad women were cavorting about upon the creaking boards of the stage, whilst the audience, a predominantly male assemblage made up of day-labourers, harbour rats, and an occasional top-hatted, decadent toff, cheered, stomped their feet, and whistled to the accompaniment of manic piano music. As we stood inside the door, searching the multitude of faces for that of our quarry, I was surprised and embarrassed to recognise a number of my own colleagues among the last group, proving that still waters ran deeper than even I had suspected in this enlightened age.

The detective uttered a small exclamation of disappointment.

'No sign of Hyde,' said he. 'Perhaps we have put him upon his — Halloa, there he is now.'

As he spoke, the man himself brushed past us on his way down the aisle, cane in hand, cloak billowing out behind him. After a few steps he stopped and swept the room, as he had the night before in Stürmer's, with a defiant gaze. This time, however, there was no anger, but rather arrogance, as if he considered himself master of all that he surveyed. I fought the urge to avert my face as his glance swung in our direction, lingered an instant, then moved on. Our disguises, it seemed, had stood up to the supreme test. Even so, I was racked once again with a savage, unreasoning hatred for this man and all that he stood for. That I should be so weak filled me with self-disgust, but a surreptitious glance at my companion confirmed that I was not alone in this feeling. Behind the masterpiece of make-up, behind even his own emotionless mask, I, who knew him so well, noted the signs of revulsion. Perhaps it was no more than a hardening of the glint in his one visible eye, or a slight tightening of his thin lips; certainly it was no more. But the signs were there nonetheless, and I alone could read them. Hyde struck the same primitive chord in everyone he encountered.

The new-comer removed his top hat and cloak and, there being no-one to receive them, carried them with him to a seat in the third row. Hatless, his head, a mass of shaggy black hair, swept backwards from his bulging brow in a simian crest, completing his resemblance to a creature from the primeval forest. I noted also that he walked with his toes turned inwards slightly, as Holmes had deduced before ever the two had laid eyes upon each other; could that, I wondered, be the reason for the impression which I received of some nameless deformity in Hyde's appearance? But it was a question left unanswered as he took his seat and dropped out of sight amidst the much taller patrons who surrounded him.

'We had best find seats,' whispered Holmes.

We proceeded down the aisle to the fourth row, where, as fortune would have it, we found two vacant seats almost directly behind Hyde, and squeezed in between a ragged pedlar and a muscular fish-monger who reeked of his profession. There we sat back to enjoy the performance as best we could.

I will not embarrass the reader with the details of that production, other than to deplore the things which a certain class of women will do in order to hear the sound of coins clinking about their feet. Lest we appear conspicuous by our abstention, at Holmes's insistence I joined him in tossing pennies and half-pennies up onto the stage and whistling in a manner most unbecoming our station. I thanked heaven for my friend's proficiency in the art of disguise, for if any of my West End acquaintances had recognised me during those moments I should certainly have been forced to retire from society altogether.

In front of us, Hyde watched the show for some little time in stony silence. Then, rising, he dipped into his pockets and flung a silvery cascade of shillings and half-pence scattering over the stage. The more substantial noise made by these denominations as they struck and clattered about the boards was not lost upon the dancers, who squealed and dropped to their knees to scoop up the unexpected bounty, oblivious to the protests of those patrons who wished the entertainment to continue. Hyde's laughter as he watched them chasing the coins was nasty. Around us, the complaints of the ruffians took an ominous turn as the source of their disappointment became known. Faces black with fury turned upon the dwarfish creature in the third row.

'Trouble brewing, Watson,' my comrade informed me. 'You would be wise to keep your revolver at hand.'

I nodded my understanding and, slipping my hand into the right pocket of my pea-jacket, closed it over the butt of that instrument which had seen us through many a harrowing episode unscathed.

'There 'e is,'im what stopped the show!' bawled a Cockney sailor in the far corner, pointing at Hyde.

The latter met his gaze with a wolfish sneer.

'Get him!' roared a drunken voice behind us.

A square-featured ruffian who had been seated beside Hyde sprang to his feet and sent a fist the size of a ham swinging at his neighbour's head. Hyde ducked and, whilst his assailant was off-balance, brought the heavy crook of his cane down upon the latter's skull with a resounding crack. The fellow dropped like a lead weight.

After that the room erupted. Blackguards of every description hurdled seats and fought their way through the heaving throng to get to Hyde. This sparked fresh battles, and the air swelled with the swoop of canes and sticks and the solid sound of fists striking unprotected flesh whilst curses flew like chaff before the wind. The fish-monger beside whom I had been seated swung at me, but I sidestepped the swing and with the flat of my hand pushed him back into the tangle of brawling forms, after which I saw no more of him. Meanwhile, a wiry longshoreman in the row of seats behind us lunged forward to snatch at Holmes's collar, missed, and howled when his intended victim brought the edge of a stiffened hand slicing downwards like a meat-cleaver against the bones of his wrist. The detective followed this up with a well-aimed right cross to his would-be attacker's jaw. Upon impact the fellow went rigid and catapulted backwards, landing in a tangled heap amongst the kindling of his chair. He did not get up.

Hyde had disappeared during the confusion. Whilst I was looking for him, a hand closed like a steel vice over my left arm, the one which had been wounded in Afghanistan. I spun about, right fist poised to strike, only to check myself at the last instant when I recognised Holmes's Lascar face.

'He ducked out during your altercation with the fish-monger,' said he. 'I suggest that we do the same.'

We battled our way down the aisle and into the street, where Holmes stopped and snapped his head to right and left.

'There!' He pointed out a hansom which had just clattered off down the street. The illumination from the corner gas lamp gleamed momentarily upon a silk hat inside the conveyance.

A four-wheeler was passing. This time Holmes took no chances but hailed it with a coin glittering in his upraised right hand. It stopped.

'There's a half-sovereign in it for you if you can keep that hansom within sight,' he told the driver, and climbed in. I got in beside him. We began rolling just as the first police whistles sounded behind us.

'He's a clever one, this Mr. Hyde.' Holmes sat with his hands upon his bony knees, clenching and unclenching them in his excitement. His eye held a steely glint in the light of a passing gas lamp.

'I don't see how you can say that,' I remarked. 'The man came near to being torn to pieces by that mob.'

'The riot was a blind, Watson, staged to mask his flight. He knew that he was being watched.'

'But our disguises —'

'He saw through them. I am the one to blame; had I not under-estimated him, I would have had the foresight to cover our ears.'

'Our ears!'

'Yes, Watson, our ears. Of all the human physical characteristics, the configuration of the ear is unique. No two pairs are exactly alike. As long as they remain unconcealed, there is no disguise which cannot be penetrated by a trained observer. I had thought that I was the only man in this part of the world who had the ability to memorise such things, but I can see that I was wrong. That is it; that has to be it. No other explanation will suffice.'

'It seems fanciful.'

'Yes, that is the common fool's reaction to something which he does not understand.'

This vitriolic response struck me like a blow in the face. I fell silent.

After we had clattered onwards another fifty yards or so, Holmes laid a warm hand upon my arm. 'My dear fellow, once again I beg your forgiveness,' he said gently. 'You are right about my needing a holiday. When this is over, the Queen herself will not be able to keep me in London.'

'No apologies are necessary, Holmes.'

'Good old Watson!' He patted my arm.

If Hyde suspected that we were still on his scent, he gave no indication. The cab in which he was riding neither increased nor diminished speed, but kept its measured pace; it was as if he were making it easy for us to trail him, as if he had abandoned entirely his plans of losing us and had chosen instead to parade the details of his life before our eyes.

And what a sordid life it was! We followed the creature through opium dens and brothels, along malodorous piers and up narrow alleys, down fiendish labyrinths of which Dante himself had never dreamt. There was no vice which Hyde did not know, no spectacle so mean that he did not delight in it. The blackest corners of London were not dark enough to conceal his forbidden pursuits, though they were amply devoid of light to turn away the most determined of adventurers. Wherever he went, however, and no matter how low the individuals with whom he consorted in order to acquire his revolting pleasures, their reaction to him was universal; his money was welcome but he most emphatically was not. Like Holmes and myself, they recognised in him that common denominator of evil which rendered him an outsider in whatever circle he tried to enter.

Once, whilst hastening along the pavement towards one of his dark dens, our quarry was accosted by a one-legged beggar attired in the remnants of a regimental uniform, who balanced his weight upon one of his crutches as he held out a tin cup in which a number of coins rattled. Without pausing or even slowing his stumping pace, Hyde slashed at the wretch with his stout cane, fetching him a glancing blow upon his right shoulder. The cripple staggered and would have fallen had not the brick wall of the nearby building intervened; as it was, he stumbled against it and was forced to snatch at the single crutch that had been supporting him to prevent it from sliding away. His assailant continued on his way without so much as a backward glance. I had all I could do to keep from rushing forward and collaring the scoundrel, and might have done so but for Holmes, who, following along with me at a discreet distance, laid a precautionary hand upon my arm. I contented myself, as did he, with making a substantial contribution to the shaken beggar's cup as we passed by a moment later.

Dawn was a pale promise over the harbour when Hyde emerged from his final haunt and, after boarding the waiting hansom, turned his face westward once again. Holmes, who had been waiting with me inside the four-wheeler across the street, rapped softly upon the roof and we jolted off in his wake. We had held him in sight for several hundred yards when he turned a corner and disappeared behind an ancient brick edifice. By the time we rounded that same corner the street was deserted.

'Look alive, cabby,' Holmes hissed. 'He may have swung into a side-turning.'

But he had not. We proceeded at a walk for the length of the thoroughfare, at the end of which we found ourselves looking up and down a cross-street and finding no sign of the hansom which we had been pursuing. At length Holmes sighed and directed the driver to take us back to Baker Street.

On the way there, Holmes sat with brows drawn and lips compressed, saying nothing. Deciding that this state of mind was doing him more ill than good, I endeavoured to say something reassuring. I had barely begun to speak when he uttered a sudden exclamation and struck his knee with the heel of his hand.

'Fool!' he cried. 'Charlatan!'

I stared at him, wondering what I had done to arouse his ire upon this occasion. He ignored me, leant his head outside of his window, and barked a harsh order to the driver. Immediately a whip cracked, our pace quickened, and we sped round the kerb on two wheels, throwing both of us into my corner of the vehicle.

Holmes's eyes (he had torn off the black patch) were agleam, staring intently at the street ahead. 'What an imbecile I have been, Watson! I trust that the account which you have been threatening to write about the grisly business at Lauriston Gardens will present me as the imperfect being that I am.'

'I am afraid that I do not follow you.' I had to raise my voice to be heard over the pounding of the horse's hooves upon the pavement, and to hold onto my hat as the wind of our passage plucked at the brim. Gas lamps sped past at a dizzying rate, their illumination flickering inside the cab.

'It is simplicity itself,' said he. 'After he had his fun with us back at the Red Goose, Hyde had been at no pain to throw us off his trail until a few moments ago. He has not attempted to conceal from us his unsavoury appetites; if anything, he has been flaunting them in our faces. He knows that we know where he lives. Why, then, has he chosen to lose us in this manner? After we have eliminated all of the impossibilities, there is but one place left to which he can be heading, a place with which he does not wish us to know that he has any connexion.'

'Dr. Jekyll's!'

'Precisely! The curious link which binds the disreputable young hedonist to the respected doctor is the one thing which he chooses not to dangle before us. He must know that we are aware of its existence, and yet it is something he would rather we forgot. But here we are, and there is the evidence which we seek. Stop here, cabby!'

We halted near a dreary block of buildings which fronted upon a narrow street within a stone's throw of one of London's busiest sectors, just in time to see a hansom rattling off from in front of it and a stunted, top-hatted, and cloaked figure ducking through a squat door into the building.

'That, unless we have been mis-led, is the entrance to the dissecting-room of Dr. Henry Jekyll,' Holmes remarked. 'There sits our mystery, Watson. What brings him here at this hour? Money, or perhaps the urge to gloat over his night's activities in the presence of his respectable benefactor?' His lips were drawn tight beneath the grotesque makeup. 'There is wickedness afoot here, Doctor, as obvious as that fog which is rolling in from the east. But there is nothing further to be gained here, at least not at the moment. Let us retrace our steps to Baker Street before that constable who is eyeing us too closely from the corner makes up his mind to arrest us for being suspicious persons.'

'I fear that I am out of my depth,' said I when we were back beneath our own roof, inadequately illuminated by the rising sun struggling to penetrate the encroaching fog outside the window. 'Why should Hyde wish to keep secret his relationship with Dr. Jekyll, when he is so bold about his other interests?'

Holmes lit a cigarette and warmed his hands before the fire. 'That is the pertinent question which faces us, and I do not think that I am exaggerating when I say that the answer will go a long way towards solving our little problem. The puzzle is nearly complete; we lack but one piece. Now that Hyde has declared his enmity, there is only one man in all of London who is in a position to supply us with what we need.'

'I think I know whom you mean, but would not going to him necessitate breaking your word to Utterson?'

'Not at all. The credit ruse worked once; there is no reason to suspect that it will not prove successful a second time. If it should not – well, my promise to Utterson was that as long as it is in my power to keep the gentleman in the dark he would remain so. The situation now is such that I can no longer avoid a course of action which from the start was obviously the only practical one.' He straightened and threw his cigarette-end into the fire. 'And now, Watson, I prescribe a thorough application of soap and water and then bed. It has been a long night for the both of us, and we must be fresh and alert this afternoon when we call upon a quarter of a million pounds sterling.'

Six

UTTERSON CHANGES HIS MIND

The contrast between the stately dwelling in which Henry Jekyll lived and practised and the decaying structure round the corner into which we had seen Hyde vanish early that morning was startling; set back from the street, the building was separated from it by a strip of grass as smooth and green as the surface of a billiard table, with conical bushes spaced about the grounds in a manner reflecting the skill of a gardener who had spent years perfecting his art. Ivy clung to the red brick walls and shaded the spacious, sparkling windows, completing the atmosphere of a pleasant country home nestled incongruously within the bosom of the foul city. It was difficult to believe that a single piece of architecture could present two such diverse faces to the world, and yet one had but to walk a few steps to become convinced of the duplicity.

The butler who answered Sherlock Holmes's ring was of a type to match that part of the building before which we stood. Tall, elderly, with a great shock of snow-white hair and a thin face nearly as pale, he bore in his expression and carriage the proud yet humble air of one who is accustomed to serving, and who does so exceedingly well. He accepted between thumb and forefinger the card with which Holmes presented him, lifted it gingerly to within an inch of his watery blue eyes, and held it there far longer than it took to read the single name which was engraved upon it. Finally he lowered it and, after asking us in a surprisingly vibrant voice to step inside and wait, collected our hats, coats, and sticks, turned, and walked silently across the flag-paved room and through a pair of panelled doors. He slid them shut behind him with no more sound than one might make in drawing a breath.

The room in which we waited was less than cavernous, though what it lacked in breadth it more than made up for in the luxury of its appointments. Tasteful curtains muted the light filtering in through the windows. An excellent bust of Goethe done in flawless marble stood unobtrusively atop a pedestal in one corner, at the far end of a row of four solid-looking wooden and satin-upholstered chairs lined up with their rounded backs against the wall to our right. That wall and the one opposite sported the same number of oil paintings in matching gilt frames, which looked familiar; I stared at them for some time before I realised that they were executed in the same style as the one which we had seen hanging in Hyde's rooms. A gift, perhaps, from his unlikely benefactor?

'"Impressive" hardly suffices,' said Holmes – echoing, as was sometimes his wont, the very word which had just that moment come into my mind, 'the paintings number among Degas's best, and those chairs are Louis XIV. Three of them are, at any rate; the fourth is a copy, though a very good one. I should say that the good doctor is a lover of life, torn between the awesome responsibilities of his profession and station and a definite preference for the forbidden. Louis XIV represents stability and respectability, Degas adventure and risk. A blackmailer could ask for no better combination in a victim.'

He seemed about to say more when the doors glided open again and the butler returned.

'Dr. Jekyll will see you now.'

We were led through the doors and down a short, amply-windowed hallway to a plain door at the end, upon which he rapped softly. A muffled voice from within bade him enter. He did so, remained long enough to announce us, and, after stepping aside to allow us entrance, withdrew, drawing the door shut behind him.

We were in a study, three walls of which, save for the door, were lined from floor to ceiling with handsomely-bound volumes of every thickness – most of which, from the well-worn appearance of their spines, were there for use rather than for display. Most bore medical and scientific titles, some were legal in nature, but I noted a set of Goethe's works in the original German reposing upon a shelf not far from the door, reaffirming his apparent interest in the great poet. The one wall which was not covered with books – that which faced the door – was dominated by a pair of French windows which opened out upon a small open-air foyer paved with flags and overgrown with rosebushes. But for the grey hulk of a stone building rising ghost-like from the fog a dozen yards beyond, we might have been visiting a country estate miles from London.

'Sherlock Holmes,' pondered the man who came forward to greet us from behind a huge French Empire desk which stood before the windows. 'I don't think that I know the name.' They clasped hands.

'But I have certainly heard of you, Dr. Jekyll,' said my friend. 'Allow me to introduce Dr. Watson, one of your own colleagues.'

I accepted the doctor's firm handshake. He was a tall man, nearly as tall as Holmes himself, and remarkably well built for a man of fifty. He had a well-chiselled face and crisp blue eyes, in contrast to his manservant's watery orbs of the same colour, and his wavy chestnut hair was silvered at the temples in a way which most men hope to emulate as old age approaches but few do. His face was broad but not coarse, clean-shaven, and distinctive for its high cheekbones, well-shaped nose, and wide, sculpted mouth. If anyone could look like a quarter of a million pounds sterling, Henry Jekyll succeeded down to the last twopence. I was surprised, however, to note that he was still in his dressing gown, it being close upon two o'clock in the afternoon; but as a scientist he may have been accustomed, as was Holmes, to working upon chemical experiments into the small hours of the morning and to rising late in the day, and so I thought no more about it. Indeed, there was a purplish tint beneath his eyes and a general wanness about his appearance that seemed to bear out that hypothesis.

'To what do I owe the pleasure of this visit?' he asked Holmes.

'I understand that you are familiar with a person who calls himself Edward Hyde,' began Holmes. His manner had undergone an abrupt change from cordial to cold. There was in addition something official in his tone, not unlike that assumed by the blustering Scotland Yard detectives with whom he was accustomed to sparring.

'May I ask why you wish to know this?'

For all Jekyll's seeming forthrightness, his attitude seemed false, as though he had known in advance the question which my friend was going to ask. He was newly risen, however, and since there was no visible reason for it, I put the impression down to deadened senses and left it at that.

'Hyde has expressed interest in a small parcel of property outside of London,' my friend explained smoothly. 'He left your name as a reference. We have been engaged by the seller to interview you concerning his ability to pay the sum discussed.'

'I see.' The doctor turned his back upon us to gaze out the window. 'It is curious that a realtor would engage a third party to conduct such an interview when he could just as well do it himself.'

'There is a substantial sum involved. Our client wishes to take no chances. When your roof leaks, you hire a carpenter to repair it.'

Jekyll made no rejoinder.

'You are acquainted with the gentleman?' Holmes repeated.

'I am.'

'May I ask in what capacity?'

'We are friends.'

'How long have you known each other?'

'A year, I think. Perhaps longer.'

'How did you meet?'

'We were introduced by a mutual acquaintance.'

'May I enquire as to the name of the acquaintance?'

'You may not.'

'Very well.' The detective nodded his acquiescence.

'When was the last time you and Hyde saw each other?'

'I think that I have answered enough questions.' Jekyll turned from the window. His blue eyes were cold as ice. 'You, sir, are a contemptible liar!' he exploded. 'Your client is not whom you say he is, and Hyde has no interests outside of London. I do not know what you hoped to gain through this charade, but I certainly do not intend to help you. Poole!' He yanked at the bell-cord which hung over the desk.

A moment later the old butler entered. 'Yes, sir?'

'Poole, escort these gentlemen to the door. We have nothing further to discuss.'

'Yes, sir.' Poole bowed and turned to us, eyebrows raised.

'I pity you, Dr. Jekyll,' Holmes announced coldly. 'It is an unfortunate man who does not recognise a friend when he sees one. Come along, Watson.' He spun upon his heel and left a step ahead of the venerable manservant.

'Well, Watson?' said my companion when we were in a cab and on our way home once again. 'What do you make of this latest development?'

'I was not aware that it was a development,' said I.

'Oh, but it most certainly was! How do you suppose Jekyll saw through our ruse?'

'I should think that Hyde told him of our earlier meeting.'

'It is of course possible. But how could Jekyll be so certain that his friend has no interests outside of London?'

'The same answer?'

'If so, then the two are closer than brothers, for the doctor to be so intimate with every detail of Hyde's life. Such intimacy, I think, would destroy the blackmail theory, since it's hardly likely that he'd expect the man who is bleeding him to confide in him. Also, what theory have you formed that will explain Jekyll's delay in exposing our little falsehood?'

'I have none,' I admitted.

'Information, Watson! He hoped by playing along with us to find out how much we had learnt, else he would have denounced us immediately. That explains the purpose of Hyde's visit this morning. He foresaw our calling upon the doctor and directed him to learn what he could of the threat which we represented.' He rubbed his hands. 'This case has taken on more facets than a brilliant. It is perhaps the most stimulating in which I have taken part. But we have a visitor.'

We had stopped before 221, and Holmes's attention was centred upon the window of our lodgings, in which there was a light. An angular shadow paced nervously to and fro beyond the drawn blinds.

'Utterson!' greeted Holmes, once we had mounted the steps and entered. 'I thought that I recognised that stooping posture. What service can we render?'

It was an agitated lawyer who stalked up to us as we removed our coats; his eyes flashed and his gaunt cheeks, normally pallid, seemed to glow like a railroader's red lantern. His rage was evident. His first words, however, were cryptic.

'My cousin was mistaken!' he snapped.

Holmes raised his eyebrows inquisitively.

'He swore to me that you were a man who kept a confidence,' Utterson continued. 'You yourself testified as much in this very room. Yet no sooner had I turned my back than you went running straight to Jekyll and told all. Have you no shame?'

'You border upon insult, sir.' Holmes spoke warningly.

'Do you deny the charge?'

'I would hear more before committing myself.'

'I came here straight from Jekyll's. He knows of your involvement in the affair and has delivered an ultimatum: either I dismiss you or look for another client. I would like to know how he learnt of it, if not from you.'

'I would be interested in knowing that myself,' replied Holmes calmly.

Utterson's expression changed from anger to incredulity. 'You are saying that you did not violate our confidence?'

'I remind you that my vow of secrecy carried certain conditions. Nevertheless, Jekyll did not learn of our agreement from me.'

'From whom, then?'

'I am not clairvoyant, no matter what you may have heard to the contrary. However, it is not so very difficult to guess, since I introduced myself to Edward Hyde not forty-eight hours ago.'

'And you told him that I had engaged you?'

'I did not have the opportunity, but I should not have in any case. No doubt Hyde arrived at the conclusion himself. He is a bright young man, for all his repulsiveness. Seek not for someone to blame, Mr. Utterson; you knew that there was a danger of Jekyll finding out when you came to me.'

Utterson nodded distractedly. My friend's logic had extinguished his fury as a bucket of water poured over a blaze. 'I have done you a grave injustice, Mr. Holmes. Please accept my apology.'

Holmes waved it aside. 'Perhaps it was not so unwarranted. Watson and I have ourselves newly come from Jekyll's, where the truth came out as surely as if I had explained the matter to him. I had no other recourse.'

Mrs. Hudson came in with coffee. After we had all been served she left, and Holmes motioned the lawyer into that armchair which he had occupied during his first visit.

'You say that you came here directly from Jekyll's,' said the detective, assuming his usual seat opposite. 'When was that?'

'I left at half past one.'

'And we arrived there at two o'clock. We must have passed each other upon the way. How did Jekyll seem?'

'He was angry with me, but he made no scene. He said that he knew what I was up to, and presented me with the ultimatum which I mentioned.'

'That was all?'

Utterson shook his head, frowning at the coffee in his cup. 'I explained to him my reasons for calling you in. He was past understanding, but he insisted that I leave the matter where it lay. He reiterated his special interest in Hyde but would not say what it was. Finally, he assured me that he owed no debt to the fellow and that he could be rid of him whenever he chose.'

'And what was your response?'

'As his friend, I had no choice but to agree to his demand. But that was not my only reason. Mr. Holmes, Henry Jekyll has his secrets – I'd be a fool to deny that in the light of recent events – but he does not lie. When he says that he can rid himself of this creature, I believe him. In spite of all our suspicions it appears that the affair is quite innocent. I am the one to blame for jumping to conclusions. Naturally I shall pay you for the time and effort which you have expended.' He reached inside his coat. Holmes held up a hand.

'Let your cheque-book alone, Mr. Utterson,' said he. 'This one is on Sherlock Holmes. But before you go, pray suffer a word of advice.

The lawyer had risen to leave. He paused and looked expectantly down at the seated detective.

'I believe you when you say that your friend's word is gospel. Whatever his predicament, however, I think that he is unaware of how deeply he is involved. It is a business most dark and sinister, and before it is finished I fear that more than one life may be ruined by it. I am but a humble servant, whose services may be engaged or dismissed at will. From what I have learnt of Edward Hyde, I would not file him under the same letter. The day is coming when you will regret having bowed to your friend's will. When that day comes I ask that you do not forget me.

'I shall remember,' said Utterson. 'If that day comes.' He nodded to each of us and departed.

Holmes signed. 'Those, I fear, were words well wasted. I had hoped that I might yet persuade him to change his mind.'

'Do you really think that Jekyll is headed for disaster?' I asked.

'I have said once today that I am not clairvoyant. But Utterson was deluded when he said that his friend does not lie; he could be mistaken in other things as well.' He touched a match to a cigarette.

'What falsehood has he told?'

'When he greeted us he said that he was not familiar with the name of Sherlock Holmes. Yet a scant half an hour earlier he had informed Utterson that he was aware of my involvement. In our presence he also feigned ignorance of our interest in Hyde. A spider which weaves so intricate a web is bound to get caught. Yes, Watson; disaster is on its way to the Jekyll household. It little matters whether it arrives today, or tomorrow, or a year from now. It is inexorable.'

He fell silent, and for some minute sat smoking and staring into the fire which blazed in the grate. At length, however, the shadow lifted from his brow and he returned his attention to me.

'Well, my dear fellow,' he began, 'I believe that I promised you a holiday. Be good enough to peruse this month's Bradshaw for the next train to Nottingham, and pass me my violin. I've been having trouble with the third movement in that little concerto of Tchaikovsky's, and if I can get hold of it today I shall consider it an afternoon well spent.'

But for all his pretended gaiety, once Holmes's fingers curled around his Stradivarius his true feelings came to the fore, and when he began playing it was not Tchaikovsky who received his musical attention, but the 'Dead March.'

Seven

THE CAREW MURDER

O f the more than twenty years during which I was privileged to call myself Sherlock Holmes's associate, the year 1884 remains in my memory a pivotal period in the career of the man whom I consider to have been the most extraordinary figure of the nineteenth century. Whilst I laboured to perfect my account of the first case we shared – that which I have published under the somewhat fantastic title of *A Study in Scarlet* – the man about whom that account is centred was building his reputation upon the satisfaction of his many clients and was beginning to acquire something of celebrity status. That he abhorred fame and all of the obligations which it entailed was quite beside the point, for a man endowed with his remarkable qualities and gift for exploiting them could hardly expect to escape the clamourings of society.

Just how widespread his notoriety had become we did not learn until one day in late autumn when, whilst walking home from an interview with a cockney charwoman in connexion with a kidnapping in Manchester Square, we stopped off at a public-house to share a bottle of port and compare notes. This was shortly after Holmes had exposed Colonel Mortimer Upwood, late of the Indian Army, as the culprit behind the unsuccessful 1879 assault upon the home offices of the Capital and Counties Bank, which had resulted in the death of the head cashier, and the newspaper was rare which did not carry an account of the unofficial detective's part in clearing up the matter. We had been there scarcely five minutes when a group of drunken day-labourers seated at the next table, who had not the least awareness of who their neighbours were, launched into the following ditty, which I shall endeavour to set down much as we heard it:

> *When you don't know who the villain is, nor where to find the*
> *bones;*
> *When Gregson tugs his whisker-ends;*
> *and so Lestrade and Jones;*
> *When Scotland Yard runs around half-made,*
> *whilst Whitehall quakes and moans;*
> *Then seek two-two-one-B, my lads,*
> *and ask for Sherlock Holmes.'*

The tune went on for several more choruses, but at the mention of Holmes's name he flushed, sprang to his feet, and, after flinging a fistful of coins upon the table, fled towards the door. I was forced to run to catch up.

Once outside, my self-control collapsed at the sight of my friend's distressed countenance and I fell into helpless laughter. At first he glared at me out of the corner of his eye, but after we had walked a little way the humour of the situation bore in upon him and he allowed himself a rueful smile.

'Fame exacts a wearying price, Watson,' he observed. 'That little tune is probably making the rounds of every public-house in London.

If it reaches the ears of Scotland Yard I shall never hear the end of it.'

'It is a cross which you must learn to bear,' said I, wiping away my tears of mirth. 'Surely you did not hope to retain your anonymity for ever.'

'I must confess that I had harboured such a wish. But the business may yet turn out to some advantage, if it leads to new adventures. I detest idleness with every fibre of my being.'

'Take care,' I admonished; 'it has been nearly a year since your last holiday.'

'Would that it may be that long before my next!' he cried. 'Really, Watson, Nottingham was rather a poor choice of locations for one of my active temperament.'

'On the contrary, it was an excellent choice. Have you forgotten how near you were to a complete breakdown when we left?'

'And have you forgotten how near I came to clambering up the walls of our quaint little cottage before we returned? When will you learn that my sole relaxation is in my work? Halloa, they're crying murder!'

Like a bird-dog who had stumbled upon a scent, Holmes perked up as a newsboy came into view round the corner, waving a newspaper and crying:

'Murder in Westminster! Eye-witness account of last night's bludgeoning of Sir Danvers Carew! Murderer identified! Thank you, sir.'

The boy pocketed the coin which Holmes had given him and handed him a copy of the newspaper.

'Listen to this, Watson!' said Holmes as the youth wandered off, hawking his product. He proceeded to read the following excerpt:

SHOCKING MURDER OF AN M.P.

London society has been staggered by the sudden and ferocious death last night of Sir Danvers Carew, member of Parliament, noted philanthropist, and familiar figure at

Buckingham Palace, during a late evening stroll along the left bank of the Thames in Westminster. Police were summoned to the spot at two o'clock this morning by Miss Evelyn Willborough, a maid in the employ of Mr. Jeffrey McFadden of Millbank who claimed to have witnessed the deed whilst gazing out her bedroom window. There they found Sir Danvers's broken body, horribly mutilated, stretched out upon the path beside the shattered half of a cane said by the maid to have been used as the murder weapon.

When questioned, Miss Willborough, who seems much inclined towards romance, stated that she was seated at her window at about eleven o'clock prior to retiring, and musing at the moonlit path beyond, when she saw a chance meeting along the walkway between Sir Danvers and another man, smaller and meaner in appearance. Sir Danvers, she said, bowed and spoke softly to the other, gesturing as if enquiring his way, whereupon without provocation the other man, whom she recognised as a Mr. Hyde who had in the past had some business with her master, flew into a rage and smote Sir Danvers a terrible bow with his cane. The old gentleman fell, and before he could rise the said Mr. Hyde trampled him under foot and rained blows down upon him with the heavy crook of the cane. At this point, according to her own account, the maid fainted dead away and did not awaken until two o'clock, when, seeing that Sir Danvers lay unmoving and that his assailant had fled, she summoned the police.

Hyde is described as a small man, nearly a dwarf, with a large head and narrow features...

'Good heavens!' I cried. 'Holmes, you don't suppose that this Mr.

Hyde is the same man who –'

'It can be no other,' he broke in. His eyes had taken on the hard glint which I knew so well. 'The description is quite specific. I knew this was coming, Watson. Did I not warn Utterson that more than one life might be the forfeit if he called me off the case? My only surprise is that it has taken this long for Hyde to tip his hand. Wait here, Watson.'

We were in front of our building. Holmes thrust the newspaper into my hands and ducked inside, only to return a few moments later with something in his hand. 'Put this in your pocket,' he directed, handing me my revolver. 'You may find need for it. I have brought my own as well.'

'Where are we going?' I asked, putting away the weapon.

'To beard a murderer in his den. Cabby!' He threw up a long arm to hail a passing hansom, which stopped a few yards down the street. 'Soho Square, cabby, and hurry!' barked the detective as we clambered aboard. We were rolling almost before my foot cleared the pavement.

'It is a circumspect account,' Holmes said, indicating the newspaper in my lap. 'The police know more than they are telling.'

'How can you tell?'

'The detective assigned to the case, an Inspector Newcomen, is quoted at some length later on in the column, yet he avoids the usual platitudes mouthed by Scotland Yard's finest when they are all at sea. I've learnt that they are most reticent when a suspect's capture is imminent. They boast loudest when baffled. I should not be surprised if we are not the first visitors whom Hyde has had today.'

Holmes spoke the truth, for a lean young constable was stationed at the door of the house in which Hyde kept his rooms. He refused us entrance, after which he and Holmes argued at some length until a tall, burly Scotsman attired in a shining billcock and ankle-length grey ulster appeared upon the threshold. He wore a reddish moustache trimmed in military style and had a pair of close-set, steely eyes with which he glanced sternly from one to the other of us.

'What is the meaning of this, Trumble?' he demanded of the constable in a clipped tone. 'Who are these fellows?'

Holmes introduced us. At the sound of the unofficial detective's name the big man stiffened. 'Sherlock Holmes,' he repeated distastefully. 'I know your reputation. The newspapers delight in invoking your name at the expense of Scotland Yard. There is a public-house ditty going about –'

'Which I did not write,' Holmes finished. 'Had I done so, both scan and meter would have benefitted by my intervention. But that is neither here nor there. You, I take it, are Inspector Newcomen, in charge of the investigation into the Carew murder?'

'I am, and I am also curious to know how it is that you knew that, and how you found me here when even the Yard has not been informed of this development in the case.'

As he spoke, the front door opened again and the sober figure of G. J. Utterson stepped out of the house. His eyes widened ever so slightly upon seeing Holmes and me.

'Ah, Mr. Utterson,' greeted my companion. 'I am not surprised to find you here, though I suspect that you were not prepared to see me. There is the answer to your question, Inspector: Utterson and I have done business together, and at that time his slight acquaintanceship with Mr. Hyde became known to me. I thought that he would come to you once he had learnt of the tragedy which took place in Westminster last night.'

'I did not come to him,' corrected the lawyer. There was agitation upon his features, as if he feared that something might come out of this meeting which he would rather avoid. 'Sir Danvers was a client of mine, and a letter to me was found this morning amongst his effects. I was out most of the day, but half an hour ago I returned to find the Inspector waiting for me, and once he told me of the occurrence I of course offered to take him to that address which Hyde had given me. I – I mentioned that Hyde and I had met once or twice, quite by accident.' He looked imploringly at Holmes; I divined that he was swearing him to secrecy concerning Henry Jekyll's part in the affair.

My companion took the hint. 'And when you got here you found, of course, that the bird had flown the coop.'

'I do not think that that is any of your affair,' snapped the Inspector.

'It is every man's affair to see justice prevail,' returned Holmes. 'I am familiar, Inspector, with this man Hyde. He is a creature both clever and ruthless, which is a dangerous enough combination, and it is highly unlikely that he would remain in residence once his connexion in this dark business became known. You found, no doubt, that he had packed his things and burnt his papers?'

Newcomen started, then quickly recovered. He had not been swift enough, however, to conceal the evidence that Holmes had surmised correctly.

'You are treading upon official police business,' said he. 'I must ask you to leave. If you do not, Trumble, here, will see to it that you are removed forcibly. Which shall it be?'

'You are refusing my offer of assistance?' Holmes asked.

The Inspector eyed him haughtily. 'I have no doubt that there are some detectives who would welcome your assistance, but I am not one of them. The matter is open and shut. No man departs without leaving tracks. I shall have Hyde behind bars within a fortnight, and I shan't be thanking anyone but myself for the deed. Good day, gentlemen.'

'Are you finished with me, Inspector?' Utterson asked.

'I am if you've told me everything you know about Hyde,' Newcomen replied.

'I have.'

'Then you are free to go, and thank you for your help. Shall I have Trumble whistle for a cab?'

'No, thank you. If Mr. Holmes and Dr. Watson have no objections, I shall ride with them.'

Newcomen opened his mouth to respond, then appeared to think better of it and snapped it shut. He spun around and tore open the door. 'Come along, Trumble. We have a search to complete.' The door banged shut behind them.

'Now that you have made me your accomplice in concealing evidence,' Holmes told Utterson once we were all in a four-wheeler and rolling towards the lawyer's address, 'I hope that you have something of importance for me.'

'I think that you will understand my actions once I have shown you what I have,' said the other, looking out of the window.

Utterson kept a bachelor house in the city, where he lived and practised his profession. There he led us upstairs to his business-room, a spartan chamber lined from floor to ceiling with shelves of lawbooks and furnished with a glossy desk, two high-backed armchairs upholstered in buttoned leather, and a black metal safe which rested upon steel casters in a darkened corner. He lit a lamp, crouched before the safe, and unlocked it with a key which dangled from his watch-chain. From its recess he drew a folded sheet of paper and, standing, handed it to Holmes.

'I lied to Newcomen when I said that I had not heard of the murder until he told me,' he said. 'On the way to my club this morning I overheard a pair of workmen talking on a corner. One of them had come upon the scene of the crime shortly after the police arrived, been questioned and released. He mentioned Hyde. I went straightaway to Jekyll's and confronted him with the revelation. He gave me this letter.'

Holmes unfolded the paper. I glanced at it over his shoulder. It was written in an uneven, upright hand and was mottled with many blotches, as if the writer had been in a great hurry.

My dear Dr. Jekyll [it ran],

You, whom I have long so unworthily repaid for a thousand generosities, need labour under no alarm for my safety, as I have means of escape upon which I place a sure dependence.

Your obedient servant,

Edward Hyde

'When did he say he received this?' asked Holmes, looking up.

'This morning, by messenger,' said Utterson.

'Was there an envelope?'

'I asked Jekyll. He said that he burnt it without thinking.'

Holmes held the paper up to the light and studied it for some moments in silence.

'Foolscap,' he announced at last, lowering it. 'A common enough type, though far from cheap. The top half has been cut away with several snips of a pair of very dull scissors; notice the puckered edge. A letterhead, most likely. The handwriting reflects determination and a certain amount of breeding, despite attempts to disguise it.'

'Why ever should he attempt to disguise it?' asked the lawyer.

'That is the latest in a long line of questions which this entire affair has brought to light. May I keep this?' He folded the letter and prepared to put it in his pocket.

Utterson appeared ill at ease. 'Please do not misunderstand me –' he began.

'Oh, very well, if I have not earned your trust after all this time –' Holmes thrust the paper towards the lawyer.

'It is not that. Jekyll gave me the letter to do with as I wish, and I do not see how public exposure of his relationship with the brute Hyde can possibly benefit the official investigation into the Carew murder; it can only serve to drag a respected name through the mud to no good purpose. I would breathe easier knowing that this document was secure in my safe.' He accepted the letter and locked it away.

'It is too late for that,' snapped the detective. 'Or had you not noticed that one respected name is already being slung about in connexion with murder most foul? How did Jekyll seem when you saw him?'

'Remorseful, to be sure. He said that he had first heard of the tragedy from the cries of the newsboys in the nearby square. The letter must have seemed a great mystery before that.' He frowned. 'There was one strange thing, though I suppose that it can be explained by his disturbed state of mind.'

Holmes pounced upon it. 'What was that?'

'Well, as I have already remarked, he said that the note was delivered by hand. But on my way out, when I asked his butler, Poole, to describe the messenger, he informed me that no such person had called. Can you explain that, Mr. Holmes?'

'It is certainly singular,' said the other, deep in thought.

'And yet there is the letter to prove that such a delivery was made.'

Holmes made no response to that. 'Leaving Jekyll for the moment,' he said, 'can you tell me what that – what Inspector Newcomen found in Hyde's rooms?'

Utterson offered us each a cigar from an antique box atop his desk. We declined. Shrugging, he selected one, nipped off the end with his clippers, and, raising the chimney of the desk lamp, leant forward to ignite it. 'That in itself is singular,' said he, puffing away. 'The most damning bit of evidence, of course, was the other half of the cane with which the murder was committed – a cane which, it grieves me to admit, I presented to Henry Jekyll upon the occasion of his forty-second birthday. Outside of that, I am afraid that the pickings were poor. Hyde had, as you surmised, packed his belongings and departed in what seemed a great hurry, leaving behind nothing which might give us a clue to his present whereabouts. This of course came as no surprise. But Newcomen was puzzled to find that the scoundrel had burnt his cheque-book.'

'His cheque-book?'

'The charred stub was found amongst the ashes in the grate, of which there was a considerable lot. He must have spent most of the night just burning his papers. The man must be mad, else why should he destroy the funds which are so crucial to his escape?'

'Why, indeed?' returned the detective. 'Each day this case presents another interesting handle. I should be eager to grasp one if you will but engage me to do so.'

Utterson shook his head gravely. 'That is one thing which I cannot do, Mr. Holmes. Jekyll is no longer a part of this affair, and its outcome is of little interest to either of us. Hyde's apprehension will not bring back Sir Danvers. You may do as you wish, but do not count upon any assistance from me.'

'I said earlier that justice is in every man's interest.' Holmes spoke coldly. 'You, a lawyer, should know that better than I. You have my pity, Utterson, but you have very little else. No man is an island, immune to the ravages of a malevolent sea.'

'I think that you had better leave.' Utterson's brow grew dark.

'I quite agree. The atmosphere in this room is stifling. Good day.'

'Are we giving up?' I enquired of my companion on the way home.

'What other option do we have?' he snapped. The profile he presented against the window of the four-wheeler was taut with anger and frustration. 'Jekyll is a liar, Watson. He is more deeply involved in this business than Utterson suspects.'

'How do you know that?'

'He told his friend that the boys were crying the news of Sir Danvers' murder outside his window this morning. Yet the morning papers carried nothing of the incident; I know that because I read them before breakfast. He knew of the murder before a breath of it had reached the general public.' His attention was fixed upon the grey scenery sliding past the window. 'Gaze carefully over that maze, Watson. Somewhere out there a murderer lurks, and he will remain free so long as you and I are manacled by lack of co-operation from officialdom and the principals involved. He is too canny for Scotland Yard, yet too impulsive to stay out of trouble for long. A beast who once tastes blood will do so again. No, by thunder!' He smacked the side of the conveyance with the edge of his first. 'By all that is holy, we will not give up!' He turned then, and the eyes which confronted me shone like twin blades of steel. 'From this time forward, Doctor, you and I shall maintain a constant vigil. Though our ears ache from eavesdropping upon others' private conversations and our eyes grow bloodshot from scanning the columns of every newspaper in London, we shall not surrender the search.'

'And what will we be looking for?'

'We won't know that till we find it. But Hyde's autograph is unmistakable.' His eyes turned inwards and he smiled grimly. 'So this is your game, is it, Mr. Hyde? To lie low, and wait for the minions of the law to slacken their grip? Well, it is a game which more than one may play. A game, if you will, of Hyde-and-go-seek.' And with these words he trailed off into a fit of mirthless laughter which chilled the very marrow of my bones.

Eight

A CHARMING CLIENT

I have heard better violin solos at a third-form recital,' remarked Sherlock Holmes bitterly as we climbed the seventeen steps to our lodgings one evening early in 1885.

I had known that some comment of the sort was approaching, as my companion, to whom few things afforded such genuine pleasure as a bow being expertly drawn across four strings of catgut, had sat stony-faced throughout the musical performance which we had gone to hear earlier, and had remained silent all during the journey back by hansom. An excellent musician himself, Holmes was not ashamed to enter into raptures over a truly superb recital, but when a performer fell beneath his expectations no critical declamation was more damning than lack of comment upon his part. This saddened me – not because of the performance, which had indeed been dreadful – but because I had hoped that an evening of entertainment would help to take his mind off the subject which had been consuming his every waking moment for nearly three months, that of the murderer, Edward Hyde. Nothing had been heard of the blackguard in all that time; it was as if he had vanished from the face of the earth, creating a stagnant situation which had not made Holmes an easy man to live with of late. Now he would be more irritable than ever, and it was in these moods that the accursed needle took on a special glitter for him.

My mind was racing with designs whereby I might yet divert his thoughts into less dangerous channels when he opened the door to our rooms and, once the gas jet had been ignited, spotted the stick leaning against the fireplace.

'Aha!' he exclaimed, striding forward and seizing the item. 'We have a visitor. Mrs. Hudson has retired early, or she would have told us of him.'

'Who do you suppose it was?' I asked, removing my outer garments and draping them upon their hook. Inwardly I was elated, for the problem of finding out to whom the stick belonged seemed just the thing to occupy his active mind in lieu of cocaine.

'A tall man, to be sure,' said he, standing with the stick held upright at his side. 'You see that I can lean upon it without stooping. It is quite hefty, yet well balanced; it has not, therefore been loaded, but rather is constructed to support a substantial amount of weight if need be. This leads us to the conclusion that the owner is heavy of build.' He reversed the ends and, holding it thus, fished his lens out of his pocket and studied the brass ferrule in the light of the jet. 'Interesting. The metal is like new, whilst the grip is shiny from much handling.'

'Perhaps the ferrule has been replaced,' I suggested.

'I suspect not. A man who prizes a stick that highly would also have taken pains to touch up this spot near the end, where the enamel has been chipped off in a collision with some low object, possibly the rung of a chair. I would venture to say that he is in the habit of gripping the item without doing much walking with it. A sedentary fellow, this. He is, of course, given to deep thought for long periods of time.'

'How did you arrive at that?'

'The fact is self-evident. A man accustomed to remaining stationary, his only action being to twist his hands about the grip of his stick, has little recourse but to ponder some problem or other. Do my deductions amuse you?'

I had started to smile, but in the face of his displeasure I composed myself. 'I am sorry,' said I. 'Except for the heavy build and the constant state of lethargy, you seem to have described yourself quite accurately.'

He made no response to that but stared at the stick for another fraction of a second, something startling dawning over his countenance. Suddenly he slashed the object downwards and struck the floor with a report that must have driven Mrs. Hudson, sleeping elsewhere upon the premises, bolt upright in bed.

'Come out of there, Mycroft,' he cried triumphantly in the direction of his bedroom door. 'I know that it is you.'

Before I had time to assimilate the new knowledge which his words carried, the door opened and in stepped Mycroft Holmes, Sherlock Holmes's elder brother.

Those who have read the two accounts in which the senior Holmes played a principal role – those which I have published under the titles 'The Greek Interpreter' and 'The Adventure of the Bruce-Partington Plans' – will recall that Mycroft was a much larger man than his brother (in truth, he was obese), but that his face was not unlike the hawkish countenance of his more famous junior in spite of its fleshiness. At no time, however, were the physical similarities more pronounced than in that moment, when our visitor came into the circle of gas light and confronted his brother, extending to him a huge, fat hand; in profile, the two resembled a pair of predatory birds squaring off over a fresh kill. Then Mycroft spoke, and the genuine affection which permeated his soft rumbling voice dispelled any illusion of serious rivalry.

'It's high time, Sherlock,' said he as the other's bony hand disappeared inside his own paw. 'When I left that stick there for you to find I imagined that you would have the answer upon sight alone. It did not occur to me that you would be forced to rely upon Dr. Watson's natural intuition. I nearly froze to death waiting in that unheated shambles you undoubtedly refer to as a bedroom.' Releasing his brother's hand, he turned and enveloped mine in the same fashion. We exchanged greetings.

Sherlock smiled thinly at his brother's good-humoured jibes. 'It is true, perhaps, that I sometimes lean overmuch upon the doctor's born catalytic qualities,' he confessed. 'I fear that your own lack of energy is an hereditary trait.'

'*Touché!*' roared Mycroft, laughing and throwing up his hands in mock surrender. 'I trust that you will forgive my little self-indulgence; when I called and learnt that you were out, I couldn't resist asking your landlady to admit me and not breathe a word of my presence to you. A game lady, she. The rates which you pay her are not enough for the things she is forced to put up with. Bullet pocks in the wall, mind you, and a mantelpiece scarred all over by the point of a jack-knife! Why not spike your correspondence like everyone else? But again I beg your pardon. When one deserts his environment I suppose that it is only natural to find fault with whatever surroundings in which he finds himself. I am sorry to note that you did not enjoy your concert tonight.'

'That is an understatement,' Holmes assured him. 'I warrant that your dinner with the Prime Minister was a more pleasant experience.'

'It was strictly business. But you were fortunate to obtain a cab so soon after leaving the concert-hall.'

'It is a shame that you did not share the same fortune.'

'Here, now,' I broke in, amazed and somewhat irked by this display. 'I am quite accustomed to being awed by one man, but when I am in the minority I begin to feel like an imbecile.'

The Brothers Holmes chuckled, as alike in mirth as they were in intellect.

'My apologies, Doctor,' said Mycroft sincerely. 'I quite forgot about you, and I suspect that Sherlock is guilty of the same indiscretion. Mrs. Hudson informed me that you were attending a concert, and yet when you returned there was no sign either in your companion's manner nor upon his countenance of that special inner peace which I long ago learnt was the direct result of an evening of fine music. Its absence was indication enough that tonight's performance was not up to his standards.'

'That Mycroft had dined with the Prime Minister was equally obvious by his dress,' his brother explained. 'You must remember that we grew up together and that he is essentially the same lazy lad – forgive me, Mycroft, but you know perfectly well that I speak the truth – who detested the idea of dressing up and going out. Knowing this, and aware of his responsible position with the government, I had little difficulty in placing the blame for his evening dress upon a dinner invitation from a personage who could not be refused. In Mycroft's case, the Prime Minister is the only one who fits the bill.'

'And surely it is no feat to deduce that a cab was handy when two well-dressed gentlemen strike out across a snow-besieged city and return home with no more than a light dusting upon their hats and coats, to say nothing of dry boots.'

'As for the less fortunate,' concluded Holmes the younger, 'you may roll down your trouser-legs, Mycroft, for they are quite dry by now.'

I sat down, shaking my head. 'I am hopelessly out of my depth.'

They laughed, and, once my fellow-lodger had remanded his own coat and top hat to the hook beside mine and we were all seated before a freshly-kindled fire with glasses of brandy at our elbows, Holmes fixed our guest with an attentive stare.

'What brings you here then?' he enquired. 'Can both your quarters and the Diogenes Club have burnt down on the same night, driving you to seek shelter elsewhere, or have the Russians landed at Cornwall?'

Holmes spoke only half in jest, for it was well known that Mycroft seldom varied his day-today routine beyond his lodgings in Pall Mall, the bizarre and misanthropic Diogenes Club, and his offices in Whitehall, where he was supposed to be little more than an auditor of the books in some government departments but was in reality so much more. Aside from these, he knew no other haunts, and it was a matter of little debate that, had he his way, he would not have even that many. When he chose to further complicate his existence by trudging over to 221B, something important was in the wind.

Mycroft's expression turned grave and he leant forward as far as his bulk allowed. He appeared hesitant. 'I do not wish to appear rude in your own home,' said he, addressing himself to me, 'but I have been instructed to speak only with Sherlock.'

'I understand,' said I, placing my hands upon the arms of my chair.

'Retain your seat, Watson.' The detective waved an impatient hand in my direction. His eyes remained upon his brother. 'Dr. Watson is a man of discretion. You may speak freely in his presence.'

'I have my instructions. There is a rumour that an account is being written for publication, a murder –'

'The Drebber case is a matter of public record.' Holmes's tone was sharp. 'He has my permission to record the details and to do with them what he wishes. If you swear him to secrecy upon any other matter he will not repeat it though the very fires of Hell threatened. What is unfit for his ears is unfit for mine as well.'

Mycroft nodded, a sudden decision having been made. 'Very well. Word has reached me that you were interested in the Carew murder case when it opened some three months ago.'

Holmes started forward in his chair, eyes bright, face taut with anticipation. 'What of it?' he demanded.

'Nothing. That is the problem. What began as a simple matter of police procedure has ended in stalemate. In three months nothing has developed which may lead us to the offender's hiding place. You knew, of course, that Sir Danvers was a favourite at Buckingham Palace.'

'I had heard something of the sort.'

'His death and the subsequent inability of Scotland Yard to locate his murderer have brought threats of drastic action from high places if something does not come to light soon. Many important positions are at stake.'

'Including your own?' Holmes pressed.

His brother smiled indulgently. 'Hardly. I do not flatter myself that I am indispensable, but the chaos that would ensue in the event of my sudden departure would be prohibitive in this case. Nevertheless the problem has fallen into my lap. Your name is not unknown at Whitehall, particularly after that Kominsky business which took place last year in the Premier's office. I have been instructed to engage you to track down Edward Hyde. That is the business which the Prime Minister and I discussed over dinner tonight. These orders come from the highest source.' He reached inside his coat and passed over a long envelope sealed ornately in red wax. I had not the opportunity to examine the coat-of-arms, as Holmes immediately broke the seal and unfolded the missive. He read it over swiftly, and looked up at his brother.

'That is your authorisation,' said the latter. 'If any official should challenge you, you have but to show that paper and all obstacles will disappear.'

Holmes re-folded the paper, took out his wallet, and inserted it among the other documents which he carried. When it was safely in his breast pocket: 'Has Inspector Newcomen been advised of this development?'

'I think not. I was told that the decision was reached only this afternoon.'

The detective smiled – a trifle maliciously, I thought.

'Good.'

'You will accept the case?'

'My client is a charming one. As a gentleman I can hardly refuse.'

Mycroft rose. He was visibly relieved. 'Then I shall tell the Prime Minister that the matter is in expert hands.' He shook his head sadly. 'It is a most interesting problem. Were I not so busy...' He spread his hands, leaving the statement unfinished.

'You mean, were you not so lethargic,' countered the younger Holmes, standing and shaking his brother by the hand. 'Do not put on airs with me, Mycroft. We know each other too well for that.'

Our visitor shrugged his bear-like shoulders in amiable concurrence and stepped into the adjacent room, to emerge a moment later carrying his hat and greatcoat. 'If you should find yourself in over your head,' said he, shrugging into the coat, 'I am available at the club every day from quarter to five to twenty to eight. But do not expect me to accompany you anywhere.'

'One favour,' said Holmes.

The other paused with his hand upon the doorknob and looked back, eyebrows raised.

Holmes had picked up his cherrywood pipe and was busy charging it with tobacco. 'I would appreciate it if you would leave the task of informing Inspector Newcomen to me. It will give us something to talk about.'

When Mycroft had departed, agreeing to the request, I asked my friend who it was who had asked for his services.

'A most charming client, Watson,' said he, lighting the pipe. 'I dare say that we can consider her a fair credit risk.'

As he spoke, he inclined his head towards the north wall of our digs, which he had decorated some years previously with bullet pocks forming the initials of our gracious Queen.

Nine

THE LAWYER ENTERS A PLEA

'Well, if it isn't my old friends, Sherlock Holmes and Dr. Watson! Come, no doubt, to offer your services in the Fleet Street dynamiting case. Well, you've wasted a trip this time, for it's all cleared up, and less than four-and-twenty hours after the fact! Shows what good, solid detective work can accomplish over sitting back and spinning fine theories.'

Standing amidst the hustle-bustle of Scotland Yard's labyrinthine corridors the morning after our conversation with Mycroft, Holmes waited until our old friend Inspector Lestrade had finished crowing before he spoke.

'Good morning, Inspector,' said he indulgently. 'So you've solved it. Congratulations.'

The little rat-faced man rocked back and forth upon his heels in an attitude of supreme self-satisfaction, his fists planted deep in the pockets of his trousers. 'The culprit is behind bars this very minute, and if what he's given the stenographer checks out, it's the morning drop for him and all of his cronies. Admit it, now: your method of looking at tobacco-ash and such and putting it all together to suit some theory has its values in some cases, but there are times when fancy falls short of the mark and industry prevails.'

'It was O'Brien, wasn't it?'

An inflatable gas-bag with a burst seam could not have collapsed more rapidly than did the official detective's self-assurance at Holmes's simple query. He ceased rocking and stared at my companion as if the latter had just waved a wand and changed the dreary building in which we were standing into a pumpkin shell. Which, in a sense, he had.

'Who told you?' he fumed, at length. 'Was it Gregson? He'd stop at nothing to –' His brow grew dark.

Holmes laughed gently. 'I see that you two have not patched things up since that Lauriston Gardens business. Fear not, Inspector; I have not seen Gregson in some weeks. But I formed my opinion of the dynamiting yesterday, when I read of it in the *Times*. O'Brien was the only one connected, who had the means, motive, and opportunity to destroy the building which shelters one of our city's most influential newspapers. His relations with the Irish rebels are well known in the London Underworld. But that is not what brings us here today.'

'What, then?' sulked Lestrade. It was plain that the unofficial detective had ruined his day.

'My business is with Inspector Newcomen. If you would be so kind as to direct us to his office –'

'Round the corner, second door on the right,' interrupted the other, brightening somewhat. 'He'll be glad enough to see you, I expect, after all of this time with no action on that Westminster killing. I'm happy enough not to be in his boots right now.'

'I doubt that my welcome will be effusive,' Holmes responded and, nodding to the little inspector, took his leave. I followed.

The door to Newcomen's office stood open, so we went right in, narrowly averting a collision with a uniformed constable who was hurrying out. His pale countenance and stammered apology as he brushed past left me with the distinct impression that he had just undergone a severe dressing-down at the hands of his superior.

My first glimpse of the burly Inspector confirmed that impression. Facing the door, leaning forward over his paper-cluttered desk with his beefy hands braced against the edge, he was seething; his close-set eyes glittered like steel beads beneath the drawn thatch of his brows and his rust-coloured moustached bristled. His reddish hair stuck out all over as if he had been tearing at it. His collar was awry, his face beet-red. Our entrance did little to alleviate his sour mood.

'Who let you in?' he thundered. 'By God, I'll litter this floor with badges if just one more constable fails to carry out a direct order!'

'Calm yourself, Inspector,' said Holmes coolly. 'I am not without friends here at the Yard. I have come once again to offer my services in the Carew murder case.'

'Get out! I told you once that I'll not have you meddling in official police business. Some of my colleagues may feel that they cannot function without you, but I am not in that number.'

'There are those who do not agree with you.'

'Trumble!'

The shout was answered almost instantly by the appearance of the lanky young constable whom we had last seen at Hyde's dwelling in Soho.

'You called, sir?'

'See that these gentlemen are shown out of the building... none too gently.'

Trumble nodded and moved forward to take Holmes by the arm. The unofficial detective side-stepped the maneuver neatly, reached inside his coat, and drew out the missive which Mycroft had given him, flipping it open beneath the Inspector's nose.

All the colour fled from Newcomen's face as his eyes fell to the crest at the bottom of the letter.

'That will be all, Trumble,' said he in a much-subdued voice. 'Close the door on your way out'

'If you say so, sir.' The youthful officer sounded perplexed but turned upon his heel and withdrew obediently, pulling the door shut behind him.

The Inspector indicated a pair of straight wooden chairs in front of his desk, which we accepted. He sank into his own seat as if his legs were no longer steady enough to support him.

'I under-estimated you,' said he quietly.

'Many do,' remarked my companion. He returned the letter to his pocket. 'It is an attitude which I encourage, for it gives me a definite advantage. Now, Inspector; what have you found out about friend Hyde?'

'Very little, or you would not be here now.' Having resigned himself to the situation, the official detective warmed to the subject. 'The man is a monster; that much is obvious, even aside from the brutality of his crime. We have sought out every one of his associates who is available and pumped them for information. What I have heard about the man is abominable. He appears to have nurtured the very lowest form of acquaintanceships, yet there is not one among those whom we have interviewed who was not appalled at his excesses. Conscience is a stranger to him, cruelty a way of life. I tell you, I have heard tales that would make your hair stand on end. But of his present whereabouts I have been able to glean nothing.'

'Perhaps his friends are protecting him,' I suggested.

He shook his head. 'The man has no friends. It's a suspicious lot, this crew with whom I have spoken, and more than a few of them have their reasons to distrust the police, but I got the impression that, had they known his hiding-place, they would have given it up like that.' He snapped his fingers. 'It's not just the reward which we have offered for Hyde's capture, either. There is about the man an atmosphere of cruelty and hatred from which all men shrink, no matter how vile their own station. Yet with all of this against him he has still to surface.'

'Have you the murder weapon here?' Holmes enquired.

Newcomen fumbled amongst the papers heaped atop his desk and drew out a stout wooden cylinder perhaps eighteen inches long, with an iron ferrule at one end. The other end was a broken shard. Holmes accepted it and studied it closely.

'Recognise it, Watson?' said he, showing it to me.

'It certainly looks like the cane with which Hyde threatened us at Stürmer's,' said I.

'So it does. Without doubt it has been shattered by a violent blow of some sort. I think that we may safely refer to it as the instrument by which Sir Danvers Carew met his untimely death.' He returned it to the Inspector.

'You had doubts?' asked the other.

'I doubt nothing until I have seen the evidence. It is an easy thing, however, to leap to conclusions when confronted with so disturbing an aberration as murder. Newspaper accounts are seldom to be taken upon face value.'

The Inspector fidgeted beneath Holmes's steady gaze. 'Yes. Well, I have given you everything we have. Except, of course, the charred cheque-book, about which you doubtless already know. I hope that you will not forget us should anything develop at your end. Not that I think it will.'

'Oh, but it has.'

'It has?' The expression upon the Scot's haggard countenance was not as appreciative as it should have been, under the circumstances. 'What?'

'A pattern. Don't you see it? Sir Danvers' murder, the trampling of the little girl, the assault upon the crippled beggar – remind me to tell you about that last later, it's a remarkably repelling narrative – every one of Hyde's known crimes has sprung from no motive other than malice. Personal profit does not enter into it, nor even revenge. As far as my own extensive knowledge of the history of crime reaches, it is without precedent. The grisly excesses of Burke and Hare would not have taken place had not the impossibly restrictive medical practices of the day placed a premium upon the carnal goods they delivered. Betsy Frances and Mary Tirrell might be alive today had not the fears of young George Hersey driven him to introduce massive doses of strychnine into their delicate systems. The will to survive turned the members of the pioneering Donner party into murderers and cannibal...' One by one Holmes ticked off examples from his extensive studies into the black side of human nature with his right index finger upon his left palm, until it began to appear as if even a hardened soul like Newcomen might grow pale, whereupon the unofficial detective abandoned his reverie. 'The point is, Inspector, that we are dealing with evil personified. The popular explanation that Hyde is mad simply will not do. I have met the man, and I assure you that there is none saner.'

'And your conclusion?'

'I have none as yet. I am convinced, however, that somewhere in that hypothesis lies the key to the entire affair. Perhaps with both of us working upon it from opposite ends –'

'I shall thank you not to explain my job to me, Mr. Holmes.' The Inspector's manner now was icy. 'But I appreciate your efforts, inconclusive as they are. Should by chance you stumble upon something important through them, I am sure that you will have the good sense to get in touch with this office.'

'You will be the first to know.' Holmes rose. 'Good day, Inspector, and thank you for your co-operation.'

'What did you accomplish by that?' I asked my companion as we stepped from the gloomy interior of the Yard into the minimal mid-morning sunlight. There was more snow in the air.

'If nothing else, self-satisfaction,' said he, pausing to light his pipe in the shelter of a doorway. 'The memory of Newcomen's expression upon beholding my royal authorisation will warm many a cold night when I am in my dotage. On the practical side, I have made my part in the affair known amongst those who are in the best position to hinder my investigations, which may spare us some difficulty in the long run.'

'Speaking of runs,' said I, 'Utterson seems to be quite done in by his.'

I had been watching as a cab rattled to a hasty stop across the street and the long, gaunt figure of the lawyer came barrelling out, scarcely pausing to pay the driver before he took off on foot in our direction, dodging between and around the jolting vehicles which made up the traffic in that busy quarter; as he drew near I could tell by his gasping and the cherry-red hue of his face that this had not been his first exertion of the morning. He was about to be run over by a wagon piled high with whiskey-kegs bound for some public-house or other when Holmes and I rushed forward and pulled him up onto the kerb just as the horses clattered past. We helped him across the pavement to the building which we had just vacated, where he leant against the wall, wheezing and mopping perspiration from his brow with a soggy linen handkerchief.

'Utterson, are you all right?' Holmes demanded.

The lawyer nodded, panting.

I seized his wrist and timed the palpitations which I felt there against the sweep hand of my watch.

'His pulse is slowing,' I informed the detective after a moment, returning the timepiece to my waistcoat pocket.

'It very nearly ceased altogether.' Holmes's tone was concerned. 'What has happened, Utterson? Is it Jekyll?'

Again he nodded. 'Your landlady told me where you had gone.' The words tumbled out between gasps. 'I feared I'd missed you.' Drawing a crumpled scrap of paper from his greatcoat pocket, he held it out for Holmes to take. He did so and, after a glance at the writing upon it, looked up with impatient eyes.

'I've seen this before. It's Hyde's note to Jekyll, which you showed me three months ago. What of it?'

'There is more.' Utterson's breath was coming more easily now, and his complexion had regained something of its normal colour. He again inserted a hand inside the pocket from which he had taken the note and, finding nothing there, searched each of his remaining pockets in turn until he took out yet another scrap, larger than the first, and handed it to Holmes, who pounced upon it as a hound might the trail of its quarry.

'The afternoon of the day I showed you the Hyde note,' explained the lawyer, 'I was sitting with my clerk, Mr. Guest, in my business-room when my man brought in the dinner invitation which I just handed you, signed by Henry Jekyll. Guest is something of a student of handwriting, and so in the interests of curiosity I had given him the original note to see what he made of it. When he saw Jekyll's invitation he asked to examine that as well. I gave it to him, and after some comparison he said −'

' − that the two specimens were written by the same hand,' finished the detective, returning the two notes after a quick glance. 'He is absolutely right. I told you at the time that a clumsy attempt had been made to disguise the handwriting. Since according to his butler no such note was handed in that day, it naturally followed that Jekyll himself had forged it. You were in no mood to accept such an hypothesis, however, and so I kept it to myself. You have placed me in a tenuous position, Mr. Utterson; in deference to you and your client I have committed a felony by withholding evidence from the police. Why did you not come to me with this information three months ago? You have much to answer for.' He spoke sternly.

Utterson turned a shamed face upon him. Holmes held up a hand, staying his explanation.

'Say no more. You were shielding your friend. I shall not waste any more time pointing out the folly of such a course, as such lectures have already proved useless where you are concerned. The question now is, what has prompted this sudden change of heart?'

The lawyer glanced uneasily from side to side, where pedestrians flowed past in an incessant stream. 'Is there a place where we may converse in private?'

'Simpson's is nearby,' said Holmes. 'If it is not too early for you, Utterson, I think that we could all do with a glass or two of sherry.'

Our erstwhile client did not object, and when we had all adjourned to a table in the aforementioned restaurant with a bottle of the rejuvenative liquid in the centre and full glasses to hand, he began his narrative.

'My delay in coming forward with this damning evidence may seem more justified once I have explained the circumstances,' he commenced, staring moodily into his wine. 'At first, of course, I was sick at heart to think that the man whom I'd thought I understood more than any other would jeopardise his brilliant career to protect a murderer. I had feared that blackmail was at the bottom of it, but now I harboured serious doubts about his sanity and, knowing something of the disgraceful state of our leading mental institutions, I shrank from telling what I knew lest I condemn my dearest friend to a living death.'

'As time passed, however, and the spectre of Edward Hyde gradually lifted from both our lives, I began to notice a definite change for the better in Jekyll. It was as if he had been born again with all the idealism of his youth intact; no longer a recluse, he renewed all of his old friendships, returned to his medical practice, which had always been distinguished for the many charity cases which he took on for no reward other than the satisfaction of healing, and even became a frequent church-goer, something which he had never been previously. His spirits soared higher than I had ever known them, as if he had at last exorcised himself of that daemon which had threatened to bear him down into the deepest recesses of Hell and made peace with his restless urges. In this light, perhaps you will understand why I deemed it best that the entire episode involving Hyde be forgotten – his disappearance, as it were, having made up in some measure for the murder of Sir Danvers.

'It was on the morning of January twelfth that I found Jekyll's door barred to me for the first time since the murder. His butler explained that his master was indisposed and could not see anyone. I thought little of it at the time, since just four nights previously I had dined there in a small company which included Hastie Lanyon, and the evening had been one of jolly camaraderie, with no indication of anything but bright days to come. Indeed, it looked as if the two doctors might yet bridge the chasm which had kept them apart for more than a decade. I returned on the fourteenth and again on the fifteenth, and still he would not see me. This sudden return to his old reclusive ways disturbed me, and after mulling it over for some time I went to see Lanyon on the seventeenth, last night.'

At this point the lawyer's nerves seemed to have failed him, and he took a hasty sip of the dark liquid in his glass. Then he resumed, in tones heavy with meaning.

'Mr. Holmes, I have never beheld so rapid a change in a man as I saw in Dr. Lanyon last night. A scant nine days before, he had been the very picture of health; now I found myself in the presence of a man as near death as any I have ever seen. Formerly robust and ruddy of complexion, he was pale as a ghost and withered horribly, his flesh hanging upon his bones like yellowed linen from a clothing-rod. His voice trembled, and when he stepped back from the door to admit me he shuffled like a man in his last extremity. I very much fear that he will not live to see spring.

'He explained that he had suffered a shock from which he will not recover, and that there is nothing left for him but the grave. Worse, I inferred from his words that he is glad of it. When I mentioned Jekyll, crimson patches appeared upon his sallow cheeks and he forbade me to mention his name again. He said further that as far as he is concerned Henry Jekyll is already dead. That is how the matter stands at present, and I suppose that it is unnecessary to add that I spent a sleepless night before I decided to come to you.' He shuddered and looked across at my companion with a pair of eyes in which all the anguish of the world seemed to rest. 'Mr. Holmes, is there nothing you can do which will stem this tide of woe?'

'I cannot say,' responded the other, whose own wine-glass remained untouched before him. 'It may already be too late.'

'I know that I have no right to ask for your help.' Utterson's voice now was a faint whisper. 'But I have been on this earth fifty years, and I shall not live to make another friend like Jekyll or Lanyon. I do not wish to spend the rest of my existence alone.'

When there was no response, the lawyer stood and, after murmuring a farewell to each of us, turned to collect his hat and coat. Holmes leant forward and snatched his sleeve. He turned back. Their gazes locked.

'I shall do what I can, Mr. Utterson,' said the detective. 'I can promise no more.'

'God bless you, Mr. Holmes.' Utterson's eyes glistened with moisture. Then he left the restaurant.

'Watson, are you willing to try your hand as a detective?' asked my companion on our way out.

'Whatever skills I may possess in that line could never hope to equal your own,' said I, my curiosity aroused by this strange request.

'You cannot know that until you try.'

'What is it that you wish of me?'

'A cross-examination.'

Confidence overtook me. During my brief career as a military surgeon in Afghanistan I had had ample opportunity to observe the regimental physicians ascertain by a circumspect question-and-answer session whether a would-be patient was indeed ill or shirking, and had myself often taken part in these interviews. I fancied myself proficient in the art of cross-examination, which in many ways is as vital to the medical man as it is to the court barrister. Here at last was an area in which I could win the admiration of the man whom I admired above all others.

'And whom am I to cross-examine?'

'Dr. Hastie Lanyon, of Cavendish Square.'

'That would require the utmost delicacy,' said I. 'If Utterson spoke the truth, his death is imminent, and I should not relish the thought of being the one who brought it about.'

'Quite right.' He was in the act of re-lighting his pipe. 'That is why I am entrusting this deed to you, whose sensitivity is unsurpassed by anyone else of my acquaintance. Draw him out, Watson. Find out what Jekyll is up to. It's plain that we're no longer welcome beneath the great man's roof, and yet I feel certain that it is from his end that this affair will yet find its *dénouement.*'

'And what will you be doing?'

He got the tobacco going and drew in a great lungful of smoke, smiling impishly as he released it. 'Ah, but that is something which you must not ask me just yet. You must allow me my idiosyncracies. Here is a cab now. You remember Lanyon's address? Excellent. You have a remarkable memory for details; it is one of the things which I most admire about you. Very well, then. Into the cab like a good fellow, and I shall meet you back in Baker Street for dinner.'

Ten

The Man In The Cab

Dr. Hastie Lanyon lived in a fine old house at the corner of Wigmore and Harley Streets in the very heart of the doctors' quarter, a four-storeyed brick edifice which dwarfed most of the other buildings in the neighborhood and looked as if it had been erected during the reign of James I. The stone steps leading up to the front door had been worn hollow by the countless pairs of feet which had trod them over the years. Scarcely had I made use of the brass bell-pull when the iron-clamped oaken door swung inwards as on a pivot and I found myself face to face with an expressionless manservant whose thick features overlain with scar-tissue made me suspect that he performed double-duty as a bodyguard. I catalogued this information in my memory for future reference.

'Yes?' His voice put me in mind of sandpaper being dragged listlessly across a stubborn piece of wood.

'My name is Dr. Watson,' said I, presenting my card. 'I would like to speak with Dr. Lanyon.'

He made no motion to accept the card. 'Dr. Lanyon is very ill.

He can see no-one.' The door began to close. I borrowed a leaf from Holmes's book and inserted my foot behind the threshold. The heavy door nearly crushed it. I bit my lip to keep from crying out.

'I think that he will see me.' Somehow I managed to keep the strain from my voice. 'It is about Dr. Jekyll. More specifically, it is about Dr. Jekyll and Mr. Hyde.'

It was a moment before the butler responded. 'Wait here, please.' He began again to close the door, paused and glanced meaningfully downwards. I withdrew my foot. The door slid into its casing with a reverberating boom.

I took advantage of the time left me to sit upon the top step and massage my injured appendage, and was thus engaged when the door opened again. I scrambled to my feet.

The manservant's features were as blank as before. 'Dr. Lanyon will see you now.' He stepped aside.

I was led down a shallow corridor lined somewhat incongruously with handsome modern water-colours – hung there, no doubt, to remove patients' fears that the physician's methods of healing were anything but up to the moment – and ushered into a comfortable consulting-room in which efficient medicine was much in evidence: leather-bound medical journals jammed the bookshelves and a new-looking microscope reposed unobtrusively surrounded by glass slides upon a deal table near the door, whilst an oaken filing cabinet with drawers labelled alphabetically stood at the rear of the room. The top drawer was open, and what looked to have been its contents – a dozen or so manila folders crammed with papers – were heaped high atop a modest desk before the cabinet. These were the only details which I was able to make out, however, for no lamp was burning and the only illumination in the room, aside from that provided by the flames in a huge old fireplace at the other end, was that sunlight which filtered through the heavily-curtained window, leaving the corners in shadow.

A man who had been seated in a stuffy leather armchair in one of these corners rose unsteadily at my entrance and stood there swaying. He made no attempt to shake hands and so I did not offer mine. His features were indiscernible in the gloom.

'Is there any reason why I should know you, Dr. Watson?' he asked in a dissipated voice. There was in his speech a minute quaver, as one sometimes detects in that of an old man for whom death is approaching.

'None whatsoever,' I responded. 'We do not travel in the same circles.'

'And yet it would seem that we have a mutual acquaintance in Henry Jekyll.'

He nearly spat the last two words. Now I became aware of an undercurrent of bitterness which seemed to be the only strength he had left. He shambled towards the centre of the room, and as he did so a bar of pale light from the window fell across his features.

Death is hardly novel to one of my experience, and yet I think that I have never been in the presence of a man upon whom it was more clearly written than it was on Hastie Lanyon. He was balding, but in a manner which suggested some sudden malady rather than the systematic ravages of age, large patches of pink scalp showing here and there amidst the white. His hazel eyes were clouded and sunken, his complexion pasty-white, his full jowls, which may once have been cherubic but of recent years had taken on a bulldog tenacity indicative of a cantankerous old age, now slack and glistening with a most unhealthy sheen. Purple circles beneath his eyes told of too many nights spent without sleep, hollow cheeks of too many days without sufficient food. Utterson had been no less than correct when he predicted that his old friend would not survive the winter, but my trained eye foretold that he would be fortunate even to see March.

'I know what you are thinking,' said he, watching me from the canyonesque recesses of his sockets. 'I have no illusions about it; the rest of my life is waiting for me within the next fortnight. I am even now in the midst of updating my patients' records for the physician whom I have chosen to inherit my practice.' He nodded towards the pile of folders upon his desk. 'Which is why I scarcely have time to wait for you to state your business in anything but a direct manner.'

'May we sit down?'

Standing for him was too painful to allow argument. With a quaking hand he waved me into a curved armchair near his leather one and resumed his own seat, collapsing into it as if the very effort of retracing those few steps had been too much for him.

'I represent Mr. Sherlock Holmes, the consulting detective,' I began. 'He has been engaged by the authorities to investigate the murder three months ago of Sir Danvers Carew. It hardly matters in what fashion the trail has led us to Dr. Jekyll; suffice it to say that it has. I understand that you and Jekyll are old friends.'

Something akin to normal colouring may have stained his pale cheeks just then, but I could not be sure, so dark was the corner in which we sat. My host had made no effort to light a lamp. 'Anything Henry Jekyll and I shared which might have been called friendship exists no longer. I consider him as dead.'

'May I ask why?'

'You may ask, but you will receive no answer.'

I approached it from a different angle. 'What of your friendship? When did you first meet?'

'More years ago than I care or have energy to remember. We graduated from the University of Edinburgh in the same year. Black year that, which released Henry Jekyll upon the world!' His voice shook with rage and weakness. I became alarmed for his life.

'Calm yourself,' said I. 'I understand that differences arose between you and Jekyll something over a decade ago. What caused the breach?'

He hesitated before answering. Then, casually: 'Oh, you know, a clash of opinions over some scientific subject. I hardly remember what it was all about. I take it that you are a medical man yourself, and understand how jealously each of us clings to his pet theories.'

'It would appear so, to have caused you to avoid each other's company for ten years.'

He made no response. I pushed onwards.

'What is Jekyll's attitude towards you?'

'I do not know and hardly care.'

'I know that you dined at Jekyll's the evening of the eighth. What has happened since then to cool your feelings towards him?'

For a moment his eyes widened in surprise. Presently, however, he resumed his listless attitude. 'Utterson, of course. He was there. He told you we dined. At first I thought that you had done something extraordinary.'

'You have not answered my question.'

'Can you not see, Doctor, that I do not wish to talk about this dead man?'

'Then why did you agree to see me?'

'I thought perhaps that you had settled the question of the relationship of Henry Jekyll to Edward Hyde, in which case I was prepared to help you lay the matter to rest by supplying you with whatever information I could. I see now that you know rather less than I do.'

I leant forward, my heart pounding. 'Meaning that you know something which we do not?'

His expression told me that he regretted having said as much as he had. His jaw tightened. 'That was a figure of speech. I know nothing which can help you.'

'I do not believe you,' said I. 'How did you know about Edward Hyde?'

'You told me, of course.'

'I told your butler that I had come to see you about Dr. Jekyll and Mr. Hyde. I did not mention his Christian name.' I stared at him, seeking to duplicate my friend's piercing glare.

He smiled, weakly and without enthusiasm. 'You cannot trap an honest man, Doctor. The name of Edward Hyde and the details of the Carew murder have been linked for months in the press. Besides, I seem to recall Utterson having asked me about him something over a year ago.'

'I congratulate you upon your remarkable memory.'

He made no response.

'You know far more than you are telling,' said I. 'I am bound to say that it will go hard with you if it comes out later that you were involved in this affair and did not come forward.'

'What care I? By the middle of February I shall be a corpse. What will the law do then, dig me up and place me in the dock?' He paused. His gaunt face softened. 'You seek the truth, Doctor; in that I sympathise with you. I can only tell you that there are laws by which a man must live lest he descend into a world where wrong is right and evil is good, a mad world which no man may enter and still call himself a man. Jekyll has broken those laws; he has entered that world. Do not seek to follow him. If you do, it will mean your ruin as well.'

For a period we sat thus, our gazes locked. The crackle of the fire and the staccato ticking of the clock atop the mantelpiece were the only sounds in the room. Finally I placed my hands upon the arms of the chair in which I sat.

'Those are your last words upon the subject?'

He nodded, a feeble movement barely discernible in the gloom. I rose.

'Ring for the butler,' said he, indicating the bell cord which hung about the desk. 'He will show you out.'

'That won't be necessary. Since you have brought him up, however, I must say that he is an odd sort of manservant for a man in your position to have.'

'He is more than a manservant; he is my bodyguard.'

'I imagined as much. Do you fear for your life this late in the game?'

'Hardly. But there is a certain visitor whom I would rather not have beneath this roof. Gregory – that is the butler – sees to that.'

'Hyde?'

He looked up at me. For a brief moment his eyes cleared, the firelight glinting off the pupils. 'Good day, Dr. Watson,' said he.

I bowed stiffly and left him alone to die.

Walking along Harley Street afterwards, I took little notice of the fact that it had begun again to snow, or that the wind had increased and was blowing the razor-sharp flakes into my face, brooding as I was over the conversation in which I had just taken part. What scanty information Lanyon had supplied was enigmatic and beyond my power to attach either rhyme or reason to it. What had he meant when he said that Jekyll had entered 'a mad world which no man may enter and still call himself a man'? Was he saying that Jekyll had gone mad? If so, why had he not told me that in as many words? And why had he turned his back upon his old friend at the very time when it seemed Jekyll needed him most? Finally, what was the shock which he'd told Utterson was the reason for his rapid decline? My thoughts made little headway, as if the bitter cold had numbed my brain as well as my hands and face. So caught up was I in this reverie that I was nearly run down when I wandered off the kerb and a hansom swept past within a few inches of my left shoulder, plucking off my hat in the wind of its passage.

I glanced up in alarm and found myself staring into the face of the vehicle's single occupant, who had thrust his head out to see what fool had come so close to losing his life through his own clumsiness. A thrill went up my spine at the sight of the narrow, wolfish features crowded into the center of the huge head beneath the brim of the passenger's top hat. An instant later it was gone, pulled back into the hansom as abruptly as a tortoise withdrawing into its protective shell. Immediately the horse stepped up its pace and the cab receded into the swirling veil of snow. But it had not been swift enough to prevent the sudden rush of loathing which overcame me the instant our eyes met. There was but one man in all of England who could spark that strange reaction, and he had not been heard from since the night he brutally murdered Sir Danvers Carew.

Eleven

I Chase A Murderer

I cannot say how long I stood there after the hansom passed bearing its sinister passenger, staring towards the snowy curtain which had descended upon it. The audacity of the man defied belief; hunted in every corner of the land, he had chosen to ride in broad daylight through one of London's most frequented neighbourhoods, as if no murder had ever taken place. I had pictured him quaking in some dank hole, loath to venture out for fear of the gallows. There was something obscene about his present arrogance, which seemed to reflect a deep-seated contempt for established order. I stood aghast at his presumption.

At length, however, I shook myself out of my stupor and cast about wildly for a means of pursuit. As luck would have it, a second hansom was approaching at just that moment; I dashed out into the street and waved it down.

I caught a glimpse of the driver's florid face, set off by a pair of massive white eyebrows, as I swung inside, exhorting him to keep the cab ahead within sight. 'You've got it, guv'nor,' said he, and we lurched into motion.

We spotted our quarry just as it turned west onto Queen Anne Street, and followed suit. Evidently Hyde was not aware of his pursuers, for his cab was proceeding at normal speed for the slippery condition of the pavement. Snowflakes swirled round us, now heavy, now light, at times blotting out the cab ahead, but always it came back into view, recognisable by the distinctive red feather which the driver wore in his hatband. We followed at a discreet distance. At Wellbeck Street he turned south. Pacing ourselves cautiously, we rounded the corner a few seconds behind him.

At this point Hyde must have become suspicious, for at Wigmore Street the hansom in which he was riding swung eastwards, describing a complete circle from where I had first caught sight of him at Harley Street. I leant out and directed my cabby to continue across Wigmore and pull over to the kerb beyond the corner.

My reasoning proved sound when, moments later, the cab bearing Hyde crossed in front of us heading west in the direction of Marylebone Lane. Our failure to follow him onto Wigmore had apparently convinced him that his fears were groundless. I gave him a few seconds and then signalled my cabby to proceed by rapping upon the roof with my stick. We turned right at the next corner and took up the chase where we had left off.

Our wheels made sucking sounds as we rolled through the slush, slowing down frequently to avoid striking the pedestrians who hurried back and forth across the street, collars turned up and heads bowed against the cold and damp. Forced to continue in this fashion, we were hard put to keep Hyde's vehicle within sight and yet not give ourselves away. Fortunately my driver appeared to be a past master at this, as the gap between the two cabs neither increased nor diminished in spite of the many hindrances.

Our machinations were in vain, however, as on Marylebone I caught sight of the killer's brutish profile outside the window of his cab looking back in our direction. Instantly it disappeared, the driver's whip was brought into play, and the hansom shot forward, snow flying from its wheels. It took the corner west onto Oxford Street on one wheel and vanished beyond the edge of a building. I rapped for speed and was thrown back in my seat as our horse broke into full gallop.

Hyde's vehicle was out of sight by the time we rounded the kerb, but the spectacle of a loiterer brushing angrily at a splash of mud upon his trousers at the southeast corner of Duke Street told us which way it had gone. On Duke we spotted it again, the cabby's coattails flying as he wielded his whip high over his head, slush and water splattering pedestrians who scrambled out of the way lest they be run down. Fists shook and epithets flew. I paid them scant attention, as well as those which were directed as us as we sped past in Hyde's wake, splashing the unfortunates anew.

A constable took notice of us as we clattered onto Brook Street at Grosvenor Square and came running, waving his arms and blasting his whistle stridently. When he saw that we were not going to stop, he leapt back out of the way of our wheels and was plastered with mud from helmet to boots as we thundered past. His whistle was choked off, he toppled over backwards, arms working desperately, and landed with a tremendous splash in the middle of an enormous puddle.

I was ridden with guilt, but there was plainly not time for us to stop and help the officer, as Hyde's cab was drawing away rapidly. I made a mental note to contribute to the policemen's widows' fund at my earliest opportunity, and quickly pushed the matter to one side.

Up ahead, an omnibus packed with passengers was just pulling away from the kerb opposite Claridge's Hotel when Hyde's cab came along, narrowly missing the ponderous vehicle as he swerved right and then left, slewing wildly from side to side across the slick pavement. By the time we drew near, the gap between the omnibus and oncoming traffic was no longer passable; without hesitation my driver whipped his horse up onto the kerb on the left side, sending pedestrians scattering. We slammed back onto the street with a jar which chipped one of my molars, and rattled onwards. I thrust my head out the window to glance backwards; behind us, the team drawing the omnibus screamed and pawed the air and the top-heavy conveyance swayed precariously beneath the shifting weight of the panicking humanity upon the second deck. I breathed a brief prayer for their safety and returned my attention to the street ahead.

At New Bond Street, that favourite of tailors and toffs, I dare say that we caused more than one near heart-failure as we cast great cascades of mud from our wheels over a number of costly suits and overcoats whilst their owners were still wearing them. The language which we heard as we barreled through the quarter, however, belonged more to the rag-clad denizens of the East End.

A roast-chestnut vendor crossing at Conduit Street saw Hyde coming and abandoned his push-cart in the middle of the thoroughfare, leaping backwards just as the cab plunged between them. He had seized the handles once again by the time we came along; attempting to avoid him, we swerved right and our left wheel caught the edge of the smaller vehicle, overturning it and showering smoking hot chestnuts all over the street. The vendor himself executed a perfect somersault and landed in a heap amongst his own wares in the gutter on the left side. Before he could get up an army of street Arabs descended upon the scene and made off with every available chestnut. My last memory of him as I looked back is of an excited figure jumping up and down in the middle of the street, screaming incoherently and waving two bony fists above his head.

By this time the occupants of both vehicles had grown accustomed to the keening of police whistles all round us, and so Hyde's driver paid no attention to a constable who was directing traffic at the Burlington Gardens crossing when the latter blasted at him and held up his hands. The cab was in the middle of the crossing when a mammoth freight-wagon loaded with fresh lumber and drawn by a four-horse team came rumbling along towards it from the left. A collision was inevitable. My own cab skidded to a halt fifty yards away, nearly tipped over as it arced sideways across the treacherous surface of the street. The driver of the heavier vehicle stood up and leant back upon the reins with all of his might, teeth bared in a grimace of determination, muscles bulging beneath his threadbare coat. His horses reared onto their haunches, but the momentum of the waggon was too much for them and it slewed sideways, slamming against a gas lamp upon the corner and bringing it crashing down over the back of the waggon. The waggon itself tipped up onto two wheels, hung there for what seemed an impossible length of time, then went on over, dashing itself to splinters on the pavement and spilling its load with a series of ear-splitting reports. The driver dove headlong from the seat an instant before it struck and landed sprawling in the street. A moment later he got up, shaken but apparently unharmed. By that time Hyde's vehicle, which had never paused, was halfway to Piccadilly.

The street was beginning to fill with people, who ignored the attempts of the harried constable to bring some order to the chaos. We steered round the wreckage carefully and continued at a crawl until we were clear of the crowds, whereupon we broke once again into gallop.

Hyde had swung east onto Piccadilly and was proceeding at a foolhardy pace for so busy a thoroughfare. Wisdom being rare that day, we pursued him at the same rate. The snow now was falling heavily in large, wet flakes which turned the pavement, already dangerous, into a sheet of glass. Most of the other traffic had slowed almost to a stop; Hyde's vehicle cut in and out among the hansoms, four-wheelers, broughams, and carriages like a needle passing through an embroidery hoop. We did the same, ignoring as always the shouts and curses of drivers and passengers which greeted us along our journey. Once, as we drew alongside of an official-looking coach, the coachman, angered already by the effrontery of the first cab, leant over to cut at my driver with his whip, only to slice empty air when the latter swerved left sharply. The momentum of the coachman's swing toppled him from his high seat to the pavement, where a four-wheeler attempting to miss him went into a skid and jumped up onto the left kerb. This sparked off a chain-reaction all the way down the street; shouts, screeches, and smashing sounds filled the damp winter air. In the distance the police whistles took on a more urgent note.

The situation at Piccadilly Circus was far worse. There, where seven of London's principal streets converge, the heart of the Empire throbbed visibly and blue uniforms were the rule rather than the exception. Hyde's cab never slackened its pace; after cutting between an omnibus and a tram-car which were travelling side by side, it described a right angle south onto Regent Street, careering violently upon the slick pavement as it did so and coming to within a hair's breadth of skinning a gas lamp upon the corner. As it was, one wheel jumped the kerb and struck sparks off the base of the lamp when its steel hub ground against it. From there the hansom continued unhampered.

We were not so fortunate.

The tramcar which Hyde had cut off had stopped whilst the driver laboured to bring his panicky team under control. Taking advantage of this situation, my own driver sped past it and attempted to duplicate Hyde's sharp turn; halfway through it we began sliding towards the left.

'Hang on, guv'nor!' came the driver's shout.

No further encouragement was necessary. I held on for dear life to the sides of the vehicle as the scenery reeled past in a dizzying kaleidoscope of buildings, vehicles, and faces for what seemed an eternity. I felt a sickening sensation of suspension. Then it ended suddenly with a deafening crunch, the world tipped, and the next thing I knew I was crumpled into a heap in one corner of the vehicle, staring up at the sky and the spokes of a whirling wheel through the opposite window.

Excited voices buzzed all round me. Beneath the buzz there was something else: an insidious hissing noise, faint at first, but seeming to increase in volume the more I became aware of it. I was reminded unpleasantly of the sound made by the infamous Speckled Band as it descended the bell-cord to do the evil bidding of Dr. Grimesby Roylott of Stoke-Moran in an adventure which I have chronicled elsewhere. I sniffed. The air reeked of gas.

Indeed, the cab was filled with it, as I noted when I looked round and found the features of the vehicle swimming before my eyes. Dimly I was able to put it together: we had broken off a gas lamp when we struck, and now the contents were pouring into the air.

Under ordinary circumstances I might have become alarmed, but now I felt a curious sense of well-being as if this were all a bad dream from which I was confident I would soon awake. With one part of my mind, of course, I knew that this was a delusion brought on by inhaling the deadly fumes, but it was the other part, that which told me that all was as it should be, which was the stronger. Lulled by this sensation, I drifted off into sweet unconsciousness.

I came awake reluctantly to find the driver's florid face a few inches from my own and his strong hands shaking me by the shoulders. So tight was his grip that I felt a sharp stab of pain in my old wound; in my semi-conscious state, however, I was scarcely aware of it, or of the urgent words which he was whispering in a voice taut with anxiety. At length he gave up his endeavours to make me understand and, throwing my arm across his shoulders, lifted me to my feet and dragged me from the cab.

The air outside was sweeter, in spite of both the crowd which pressed in round us and the stronger odour of gas as we passed the broken lamp, which had been severed at kerb level when the cab tipped over and struck it. I was vaguely aware of a man in a blue uniform at the far edge of the crowd, blowing a whistle and fighting his way towards the centre; we turned in the opposite direction and hobbled away as fast as my rescuer could manage whilst supporting my bulk. The crowd parted grudgingly before us.

Gradually my senses returned until I was able to move under my own power, albeit with the added support of my companion's wirey shoulders. We were walking fast, prodded on by the screech of the police whistle behind us.

We had passed the Haymarket Theatre and were well on our way towards Pall Mall when it occurred to me that the driver had just saved my life. I spluttered inadequate words of thanks.

'Later, Watson, later,' said Sherlock Holmes, smiling at me briefly through his ruddy make-up.

Twelve

DEEPER WATERS

'We made the *Evening Standard*, Watson.'

We had been back in our rooms some hours when Holmes, after delivering the above statement, chuckled dryly and folded the periodical which our news agent had sent up a few moments before to the lead column on an inner page.

A report, as yet unconfirmed, has reached these offices concerning a wild chase through the streets of the West End this afternoon involving a pair of hansom cabs [he read]. Although it appears that no-one was injured as a result, three vehicles are reported to have been demolished. A constable who claims to have witnessed the episode speculates that this was yet another of those incidents which inevitably ensue whenever the exuberance of youth is allowed to combine with alcoholic spirits, and pledged his support to those who would strengthen the laws prohibiting the sale of such stimulants to minors.

'I never cease to marvel at what the Press is able to do with something so mundane as the truth,' said he, laying aside the paper to ignite a fresh cigar.

His witticism was lost upon me. I glared at him above the pages of the seafaring novel in which I had been endeavouring to interest myself without success ever since our return. 'Are you not going to tell me why you were spying upon me today?' I demanded.

'My dear fellow, I had no intention of spying upon you. As difficult as it may be to believe, it was merest coincidence that we bumped into each other at all, and nothing short of a miracle that we ended up sharing the same cab.'

I shook my head and closed the book without bothering to mark my place. 'I am afraid that I need further convincing. What were you doing out there in the first place, and how is it that you came to be following Hyde when I hailed you?'

Again he chuckled. Blue tobacco-smoke curled about his head, blurring his angular features. 'That, Watson, is one of those bizarre twists of fate which occur more often in life than any of us would believe, and which all of us would be swift to decry were it to appear in a work of fiction. You will remember that I asked you to interview Dr. Lanyon whilst I attended to other business. After our parting I returned straightaway to these rooms and donned that disguise which by your failure to penetrate it I fancy was a fair one. From here, I paid a visit upon an elderly acquaintance of mine, a retired cabby who for sentimental reasons had, upon leaving his company's employ, purchased the hansom which he had driven for a decade; as luck would have it, he is moving soon to smaller quarters and was at a loss concerning what to do with his ungainly possession. I made an offer for it, it was accepted, and after renting a horse elsewhere I was set to go.

'The reason for the disguise is obvious, since I believe I mentioned that neither of us is a desirable visitor where Henry Jekyll is concerned. You see, Watson, I have suspected for some time that Jekyll is the key to Edward Hyde's whereabouts; he is the only man living whom Hyde could consider a friend, and experience has taught me that no-one may remain a fugitive for long without co-operation from some quarter.

'I hardly knew what I was looking for, or even whether I'd recognise it when I found it. But every man has his own regimen, his rails upon which he runs as faithfully as any train; I was prepared to maintain a vigil at Jekyll's home every day for a month if necessary until such time as his routine pointed in the direction I hoped it would. It is the little things, Watson, which betray us, and you should know by now that the observation of trifles is my *forte*.

'Imagine my triumph when, just as I arrived, a hansom rattled off from in front of Jekyll's house in the direction of Cavendish Square. This may be what I am after, thought I, and I immediately gave chase.'

'You were not observed?'

He appeared wounded by my query. 'Really, Watson, I thought that you had greater faith in my abilities than that.

'I had been following for some time when the hansom turned a corner and the passenger's silhouette was framed briefly in the opening. I nearly dropped my reins in my astonishment. It was Hyde!

'I suspect that my train of thought at this point closely paralleled your own when you yourself recognised him some minutes later: What manner of man is this who would risk being seen when every constable in the city has him marked for the gallows? I do not recall ever having confronted a criminal so bold or so foolish. I was still endeavouring to make some sense out of it when you happened upon the scene. The rest you know.'

'Not quite!' I remonstrated. 'Why all of the secrecy? Why did you not take me into your confidence from the first?'

'As I recall, the last time I suggested a separation you railed against it, claiming that I was in need of constant medical supervision and demanding that you accompany me. That of course was out of the question. I think you would agree that whilst one man may, with good fortune, expect to watch a house without drawing attention, two would be pressing fate. Rather than pause to explain the situation, I thought that our time would be better served if I kept you in the dark until later, when we were both at our leisure.'

'That may be so, but what kept you from identifying yourself when I hailed you? That was shabby treatment indeed, Holmes!'

He regarded me warmly for a moment, then leant forward in his armchair and patted my knee. 'Watson, Watson,' said he, sincerely. 'I apologise for leaving that impression. I would never presume to treat in a shabby manner one upon whose friendship and loyalty I have come to depend. Had I revealed myself to you, you would then and there have asked all the questions which you are now asking, and in the meantime Hyde would have been halfway across London. Come now; what would you have done in my place?' His grey eyes twinkled.

'I suppose that I would have behaved exactly as you did,' I responded, after a moment.

'Of course you would have!' He sat back, puffing upon his cigar. 'Emotion is a cross which we all must bear, but there are ways of circumventing it when it is most troublesome. Not that doing so helped us in this instance, after my own incompetence in the driver's seat cost us our quarry.' His tone was one of bitter self reproach.

'You must not blame yourself,' said I. 'Had fortune smiled upon us instead of upon Hyde, it would have been he piled up on that corner in Piccadilly. Your driving was impeccable.'

He waved aside the compliment listlessly, but a faint smile told me that his good humour was returning. 'My teacher was the best who ever lived. But remind me to tell you about Fyodor the coachman and the singular adventure which we shared at some later date; it is a most interesting narrative. Had he but been wielding the whip today, Hyde might be in custody at this very moment.'

'It's a pity that neither of us got the number of his cab.'

'Really, Watson, your comments this evening are the most unsettling mixture of honey and vitriol,' he snapped. 'The number is 5312; have my faculties slipped so far that you think me capable of missing such a fundamental scrap of information?'

I sat up. 'Do you mean to say that you have known the number all this time and done nothing about it?'

'On the contrary, the driver of the vehicle in question is being sought even as we speak.'

'By whom? We came straight home from Piccadilly.'

'We made one stop, you will recall.'

I thought. 'Yes, you stopped to speak with a crowd of ragged street Arabs. I imagined that you were testing your disguise.'

'Why should I test it when it had already served its purpose? As for those "ragged street Arabs," have you forgotten the Baker Street Irregulars so quickly?'

'I remember that they were of some use in the Drebber murder case. But surely you have not entrusted them with the task of locating this particular murderer's cab? That is a job for Scotland Yard.'

He made a noise of derision which I found most ungentlemanly. 'I make use of Scotland Yard only upon those rare occasions when they have stumbled across some information which I do not already possess. When it comes to laying my hands upon a witness or an article of evidence which is floating about this great city, I shall throw in my lot with Wiggins and his crew every time. Your disbelief in their abilities is shared by most people, and that is their main strength. A detective whom no-one takes seriously is a valuable tool. They located Jefferson Hope's cab in short order; I have little doubt but that they will soon repeat their triumph in the case of cab number 5312. That's them now, I should wager.'

The jangling of the bell-pull floated up from the floor below. Holmes unfolded himself from his seat and strolled over to the bow-window, where he stood looking down into the dusty street, hands in the pockets of his old blue dressing-gown. 'It's our man, all right,' said he. 'I must say that it's a relief to see the old girl standing still for a change. I am referring to the cab, Watson. There are no ladies in this case, thank heaven.'

Whilst he was speaking a small altercation had broken out at the foot of the stairs, in which I detected both Mrs. Hudson's Scottish burr raised in outrage and the higher, cockney speech of Wiggins, the boy whom Holmes had placed in charge of his unofficial brigade of bare-footed waifs, attempting to placate her. She plainly did not care for the youth's presence in her tidy household. But accustomed as she was to such things as indoor target practice and all sorts of strange characters parading in and out of 221B, the landlady at length surrendered to this fresh invasion, and presently the tread of two distinctly different pairs of feet was heard upon the stairs. I answered the door after the first knock.

Wiggins, his round face grimy as ever despite the cleansing influence of the snow falling outside, stood grinning from ear to ear beside a large, stoop-shouldered man with a beetling brow and a great promontory of a chin dotted with circles of sticking-plaster. He was dressed for the weather in a muffler and a worn black great coat which extended nearly to the tops of his cracked boots. His hands were gloved, the ends of his fingers protruding through holes in the brown jersey material and gripping the crown of a shabby top hat which he held before him in the manner of a supplicant. A soggy red feather drooped from the band.

'Good work, Wiggins!' cried Holmes. 'Here is a shilling for you and each of the others. Run along, now.' When the boy had left, clutching the fistful of coins which the detective had given him, Holmes turned his attention to our visitor. 'So you are the driver who eluded us so expertly this afternoon in Piccadilly. Pray come in and be seated. I am Sherlock Holmes and this is Dr. Watson, who will be taking notes during our conversation.'

Apprehension flickered in the big cabby's expression at the reference to his earlier activity, but at Holmes's cordial invitation he relaxed somewhat and took the seat indicated. He fingered the brim of his hat nervously.

'Albert Horn is my name, sir, and very pleased to meet you both, I'm sure,' he ventured. 'May I ask which of you was driving today?'

Holmes inclined his head in a humble bow.

Horn nodded enthusiastically. 'Begging your pardon, sir, but I guessed as much. You have that masterful air about you which says that you're a born handler of horses. I've driven in this city many a year, and I never saw anyone put a cab through its paces like you did today. There was one man, though, years ago, who taught me the basics – a Russian gentleman –'

'Ha!' Holmes slapped his knee. 'I might have known. Coincidences, Watson; life delivers them by the bushel. Now, Mr. Horn, there is a half-sovereign in it for you, on top of your regular fare for the journey here, if you will tell us where you dropped off your passenger this afternoon after we separated.'

As he spoke, he offered the cabby a cigar from his case. Horn took two, placed one inside his coat, and bit the end off the second. Apparently deciding that there was no way for him to get rid of the end gracefully, he took it out of his mouth with his fingers and deposited it inside a coat pocket. Then he lit the cigar from the match which I held out for him. For a few seconds he savoured the smoke. Then:

'I'm sorry, sir, but that's a question I cannot answer.'

'Cannot – or will not?' shot Holmes. His eyes glittered.

'I would if I could, sir, believe me. Half-sovereigns these days are few and far between. But when I got to the address which he gave me and climbed down to collect my fare, he was gone!'

'Gone, you say? How could he alight without your knowledge?'

'It must have been sometime when I had slowed down for a crossing and had my eye on the traffic coming the other way. 'It's happened to me before, but not when my passenger was a toff, like this time. And after him promising me a sovereign if I lost the other cab. I don't mind telling you that I was fair put out.'

'What makes you think he was a toff? His dress?'

'Well, clothes like them he was a-wearing plays their part right enough, but there was more to it than just that. A gentleman through and through he was, or so I thought till he left me holding the sack. A fine figure of a man; tall, poised, soft-spoke –'

'Good heavens!' I cried, looking up from my notes. 'That hardly sounds like a description of Hyde.'

'Rather like Jekyll, I should say,' reflected Holmes, contemplating his cigar-end. He tossed it away. 'You are certain of this description?'

'I was as near him as I am to you.' The cabby was indignant. 'I should think that I'd know a gentlemen when I see one. He come out of that door like a blooming lord and hailed me with his stick. A driver can't be too careful these days, so I took thorough measure of him before I let him in. I won't carry no ruffians.'

'No-one is doubting your word,' Holmes assured him. 'But it is curious.' He began to pace, unconsciously reaching inside his dressing-gown pocket for his meditative pipe. It was charged and lit before he spoke again. 'Where did he ask you to take him?'

'Wigmore and Harley.'

Holmes swung round.

'That's Lanyon's address!' I exclaimed.

'Yet you went past the address,' prodded the detective.

Horn nodded. 'We was just round the corner from it when my passenger rapped on the roof with his stick and told me to circle round to where I'd picked him up.'

'Did you not think that a strange request?'

'Mr. Holmes, I've driven cabs a long time, and I've taken on all sorts of passengers. Very little surprises me any more.'

'Tell me, did you notice anything odd about your passenger's voice upon this occasion?'

Horn's brow puckered. 'Yes, it seemed greatly changed.'

'Changed how?'

'It sounded much harsher. More like a grating whisper. I remember thinking that perhaps he had suffered some kind of attack and had changed his mind about visiting because of it.'

'Hardly likely. Why, then, would he turn his back upon the doctors' quarter, where medical help was everywhere? But all this is beside the point. Pray continue.'

He shrugged. 'That's all there is to tell. Not long afterwards he rapped again and made me that offer of a sovereign if I got rid of the cab what was following us. You saw the rest.'

'Thank you, Mr. Horn. Here is the half-sovereign which I promised, plus a little more which should take care of your fare. You have been a great help.'

When the cabby had departed, thanking him, Holmes turned to me. 'Well, Watson? What do you make of that?'

'I am at a loss to explain it,' said I.

'Come, come; you must have formulated some theory which will cover the facts as we know them.'

'I have nothing to offer, other than the obvious conclusion that Jekyll and Hyde switched places somewhere along the journey.'

'The probability lies in that direction, to be sure. The snow was falling heavily, and behind its veil such an exchange was eminently possible without my witnessing it. But why? Tell me that.'

'I cannot guess.'

'Of course you cannot, and neither can I, nor will I try. Imagination becomes useless when it is compelled to cross into the realm of fantasy. We simply do not have enough facts. Let us attack it from a different angle. What did you learn during your conversation with Lanyon?'

I gave him a detailed account of the interview, including my conviction that the physician knew more than he was willing to divulge. He listened in moody silence, smoke drifting lazily upwards from the bowl of his pipe. When I had finished he went over and knocked its contents into the grate.

'I think,' said he, 'that we are dining upon pheasant tonight. I smelt scorched feathers earlier and now a most delicious and familiar aroma is floating up from Mrs. Hudson's kitchen.'

'Is that all you have to say?' I was irked by his irrelevance. 'What has supper to do with solving this mystery?'

'It has everything to do with it,' said he smiling. 'An engine cannot run without fuel. How is your memory these days, Watson? Good as ever, I trust?'

'I trust. Why?'

'We shall need it to find our way about tomorrow. I should not wish it voiced abroad that Sherlock Holmes became lost upon the grounds of your old *alma mater*, the University of Edinburgh. Perhaps a dash of clear British academic thinking will show us the way out of these very deep waters in which we seem to be floundering.'

Thirteen

ACADEMIA

The journey by rail from London to Edinburgh, apart from the invigorating experience (in my own case) of viewing scenery which I had not beheld in more than a dozen years, was a physically exhausting one, with the result that for two days after our arrival neither of us stirred from our room at the inn. Holmes put that time to use placing the finishing touches upon a monograph in which he catalogued some sixty-seven common deadly poisons, along with brief case histories recounting the various methods by which all of them had been applied to evil purpose by some of our fellow citizens. Not once during that period did he allude to the mission which had brought us there, other than to state, when I pressed him upon it, that further progress was out of the question until more data became available. Inspired by the literary atmosphere, I set to work once again arranging my notes concerning the Drebber case into that chronicle which was eventually to introduce the world-at-large to the remarkable talents of Sherlock Holmes, only to find that I was too pre-occupied with the current turn of events to do justice to that tangled skein, and at length I put away my materials and settled back to read what others had written. It was a grey January day when, rejuvenated at last, we stepped onto the grounds of one of the finest institutions of higher learning which the Western world has to offer.

'Our wisest course is to find someone who knew Henry Jekyll when he was attending classes here,' said Holmes as we made our way down a well-trammelled path through a maze of students hurrying to and fro, carrying armloads of books. 'Failing that, we shall have to rely upon the University records. How about it, Watson? Does anyone come to mind who answers that description?'

'There is old Professor Armbruster,' I responded after a moment's concentration. 'He was far from young when I left; the popular jest was that they built the University round him. My latest Medical Directory lists him still among the living, but at his age that is a status which is subject to change at any moment.'

'That is easy enough to confirm.' Holmes placed a hand upon the arm of a callow student who was in the act of striding round us. The student, his arms loaded down with several ponderous volumes, stopped and glared at him in irritation.

'I beg your pardon,' said Holmes, 'but where may we find Professor Armbruster?'

'Old 'brucie?' The young man's tone was a mixture of fondness and irreverence. 'Try the medical library. Where else would he be? He practically lives there.' He inclined his head towards a huge, grey building some fifty paces to our left, its tall windows framed with branches of ivy now withered to reveal the lichen-spotted stone beneath.

'Thank you. I trust that we have not made you late for your examination in anatomy.'

'I've some time yet.' He walked away a few steps, stopped suddenly, and turned an expression of comical bewilderment upon the detective.

By that time, however, Holmes was already halfway down the path which led to the medical library. I shrugged and turned to follow, leaving the young man standing there in absolute mystification.

'Would you care to explain how you knew that he was going to an examination in anatomy?' I asked my companion as I feel into step beside him.

'When one overhears a student muttering such terms as "ectoderm," "neural tube," "notochord," and "mesenchyme" beneath his breath in quick succession as he hurries past, his destination is hardly a mystery. Quiet now, Watson, for University libraries are sacrosanct.'

We passed through an enormous pair of double doors and down a shallow corridor into a vast repository whose walls were solid with books from the dark oaken floor to the sills of the lofty windows near the ceiling. Through these, pale sunlight filtered downwards to illuminate the dusty spines of countless volumes and the hunched forms of students seated round broad library tables, lost in study. The sheer scale of the chamber, however, dwarfed them into insignificance and created a curious atmosphere of desertion. At the far end an emaciated old man was perched atop a tall step-ladder, bent over a volume spread open upon his bony knees. His head, which appeared too large and heavy for his withered old neck to support, was crowned with snatches of fierce white hair sticking out all over in stiff bristles. Thick-lensed pince-nez framed in plain gold straddled his beak of a nose. He was wearing a seedy old frock-coat which, once black, had long since faded to an uneven grey. I am prepared to swear that it was the very same one which he had worn throughout my tenure as a student. As a matter of fact, he appeared not to have changed at all since those halcyon days, aside from his shoulders, which seemed even more rounded by study than I remembered them. I was overcome with nostalgia at the sight of this rock who had refused to surrender its position before the torrent of modern history which gurgled round it.

'Professor Armbruster?' Holmes addressed as we approached, our footsteps echoing among the rafters twenty feet above our heads.

'Go away! Can't you see that I'm busy?' He spoke without removing his eyes from his book. His voice was a cross between a raven's croak and the squeal of a rusted hinge.

'As indeed are we,' responded the detective. 'We should like a word with you. It will take but a few minutes and will cost you nothing.'

'It will cost me a few minutes, and I have few enough as it is. Go away!'

'Professor –' said I.

'Can you not hear? Are you deaf as well as stupid?' He glanced down at us for the first time. His eyes of faded grey flashed behind the bottle-glass lenses of his spectacles.

'I am John Watson,' I continued. 'I studied surgery under you for four years. Do you not remember me?'

He adjusted his pince-nez and peered at me. After a moment: 'Are you the young man who ran my overcoat up the flagpole in '73?'

'Certainly not!'

'Too bad. That laddie showed promise of becoming a fine surgeon. Which one were you?'

'I was in your class from '70 to '74. I worked in the laboratory nights to earn money for my education.'

'If you were that serious about it, you should have known better than to run my overcoat up the flagpole. It cost me a small fortune to repair the lining.'

I reiterated my innocence.

'Professor,' Holmes broke in, 'I should like to question you about Henry Jekyll, a former student.'

At the mention of the name the old man's eyes glittered in recognition. 'Jekyll! A brilliant young man!' he closed the book which he had been reading. 'What is it that you wish to know?'

Holmes glanced about at the students in the room, some of whom had looked up from their studies at the sound of voices and appeared to be listening out of sheer boredom. He lowered his voice. 'Is there some place where we may converse in private?'

'Oh, very well, if you insist upon disturbing me.' The professor shoved the book back into its place upon the shelf with a disgusted gesture and descended the ladder. I stepped forward to help him down the last few steps, but he slapped aside my hands. 'I'm not an invalid, blast it! And stay away from that overcoat! I haven't forgot what you did with it the last time.' Before I could hand it to him, he snatched up the shabby black garment which had been draped over the bottom step and thrust his bony arms into the threadbare sleeves.

Half-loping, half-scuttling in the manner of an excited crab, the old man led us out of the building and across a snow-covered courtyard into the neighbouring structure. There we followed him up a narrow, creaking staircase to the first floor and pattered down an ancient corridor, stopping at last before a door which was panelled in handsome old walnut. At this point I expected him to produce a key but was dumb-founded when instead he kicked twice at the bottom right hand corner of the barricade and then smacked the panel before him with the flat of his hand. The door sprang open as if by magic.

There was a pause whilst he struck a match and ignited a gas fixture just inside the door, and then he stepped aside for us to enter.

After four years' residence with Sherlock Holmes, whose aversion to casting away anything which might prove the least bit useful to him had led to the inevitable result, I had thought that no-one lived amidst worse clutter than we, but Professor Armbruster's study (for such I immediately judged it to be) was far and away the victor in that dubious contest. As might have been expected, every available bit of wall space in the tiny room was devoted to the storage of books, some upright, others jammed in horizontally, the whole packed so tightly that removing one would not have been possible without bringing about a veritable avalanche. But this haphazard system did not confine itself to the shelves. Documents of every description – some bound, some rolled, still others piled atop one another and beginning to curl at the edges – lay about the floor and covered every stick of furniture in the room, including a battered old roll-top desk behind which stood an ancient, high-backed chair whose seat was rounded over with a number of exquisitely rendered pen-and-ink drawings of the human body in various stages of dissection. The odour of must pervaded everything, and it was impossible to take a step in any direction within the room without hearing the crackle of parchment beneath one's foot.

It was the work of a few seconds for the professor to clear off a pair of straight wooden chairs for Holmes and me, as well as his own seat at the desk, and as he filled a squat clay pipe with tobacco from a jar which he kept in the deep bottom drawer he frowned and said: 'Let's begin with who you are and why you want to know about Henry Jekyll's career at this University.'

'My name is Sherlock Holmes,' said my companion, who had taken the seat beside mine and was following Professor Armbruster's example with his own charred briar and pouch. 'I have been engaged as a consulting detective to aid Scotland Yard's investigation into the violent death last year of Sir Danvers Carew in London.'

Two matches flared simultaneously. The professor puffed energetically until his tobacco caught fire, then shook out the match and deposited it, still glowing, atop the papers on his desk. I winced, wondering if he was always that careless with fire.

'And who,' said he, 'was Sir Danvers Carew?'

Holmes stared until his own flaming vesta burnt down to his fingers. He extinguished it hastily and ignited another. This one performed its duty; he disposed of it somewhat more carefully than was the wont of our host, and drew on his pipe.

'You do not follow the newspapers?'

'Another London murder can hardly be expected to raise eyebrows in my circle,' responded the other. I noticed that his Scottish burr, previously faint, had sharpened, as if to emphasise his lack of interest in things English. 'There are so many of them.'

'No matter. I will begin by stating that Jekyll is not implicated directly but that he is deeply involved. Whatever you can tell us about his background may assist us in bringing a murderer to justice.'

'You mean that if you are able to find him, if he does not elude capture, and if the courts convict him,' said our host acidly. 'I know your English system of justice very well, you see. Well, ask away, and I shall decide whether your questions deserve answers.'

'What sort of student was Jekyll?'

'The brightest whom ever I have taught. Everything about him indicated a brilliant future in scientific research.'

'Not medicine?'

He shook his head. 'He would have made a mediocre physician at best. No diagnostic skills whatsoever. But in the laboratory he was a genius.'

'In what capacity?'

'In every capacity, but in chemistry particularly. In one session he had the elemental table down by heart; in two he was making compositions which I should not have attempted myself without first consulting the testbook. In two years he never made a mistake.'

'Can you tell me anything about his other subjects?'

'We conversed frequently in this very chamber. Civil law consumed nearly as much of his time as did science. He was interested also in literature, and philosophy fascinated him. He never tired of discussing Goethe and Schopenhauer. The insatiety of desire and the existence side-by-side of good and evil in human nature were favourite topics; you might even term them obsessions. But then students are rarely distinguished for their moderation.'

'They are obsessions which appear never to have left him,' commented Holmes. 'Have you read "The War Between the Members"?'

'I stumbled across it some time ago. I found it interesting if a trifle obvious.'

'You and Watson seem to be kindred souls upon that subject at least. It is not difficult to see that he is your disciple. What of Jekyll's social life during his time here?'

The professor scowled, pulling at his pipe. "That, sir, hardly falls within my province. What a student does when he is not in class is nobody's affair but his own.'

'Come, come, Professor. Universities are hotbeds of gossip. You must have heard something.'

'I do not think that I care for the turn this conversation is taking.' He placed his hands upon the arms of his chair. Holmes leant forward and closed his fingers round the old man's arm.

'I am not a journalist,' said he. 'My questions are not always harmless. But your prize student is in the grasp of a creature most vile, and since his life after leaving Edinburgh appears to have been above reproach, it is my considered belief that whatever indiscretion he may have committed which delivered him into this fiend's clutches took place during his stay here. His best friend will do nothing to assist him. You are the only man living who can help me extricate him from the vortex into which he has fallen. Without your co-operation Jekyll is doomed.'

The speech had its effect upon the aged academician, who relaxed somewhat and studied his pipe for some moments in silence. Holmes released his grip but remained leaning forward, his spare profile a mask of tense anticipation.

'You will tell no-one?' asked the professor finally.

'No-one,' echoed the detective. I nodded agreement.

There was another long pause whilst the smoke from the two pipes swirled about, filling the windowless room with a choking haze and causing my eyes to smart. I found myself longing for the comparatively fresh atmosphere of London at its foggiest.

'It was early in '55,' commenced Professor Armbruster in a voice scarcely above a whisper. 'The night before final examinations, Jekyll and a number of his friends went into Edinburgh to relieve some of the pressure brought about by days and nights of study. Whilst visiting a public-house, Jekyll became separated from his cronies; when after an hour he did not return, the others assumed that he had returned to his rooms to rest up for the examinations, and after a time they followed what they thought was his lead. Jekyll roomed alone, and so there was no-one to miss him that night.

'Classes were in session the next morning when he appeared, drunk as a lord, in the entrance-hall of the house in which he kept his rooms. This would not have been shocking in itself, but he was being supported by a common woman of the streets. She gave no explanation, and when Jekyll's head had cleared he retained no memory of the night before; the mystery of the missing hours, therefore, descended into the realm of vicious gossip. And what a lot of gossip there was! Everyone, including myself, was certain that he would be asked to leave the University.

'Fortunately for Jekyll, the dean was an understanding man, and though it was quite out of the question that the young man be allowed to take his examinations, he was offered the opportunity to stay on for an extra year and take them the next time they were offered. He accepted, there were no further incidents, and when he finally graduated he did so at the head of his class.

'It was a minor indiscretion, Mr. Holmes, and has more than been made up for by the brilliant advances which this man has engineered in the cause of science, I hardly think that it can do him serious harm at this late date.'

'On the contrary, Professor,' said Holmes, 'in retrospect, given the repressed climate of the times in which we live, such a tale could bring ruin to a man of Jekyll's stature. You have been a very great help indeed. Would I be pressing fortune if I asked the name of the young lady who escorted Jekyll on that memorable morning?'

The professor smiled for the first time, in a manner which he no doubt assumed was rakish. 'It has been thirty years, but I am not so senile that I would forget a name like Fanny Flanagan, or the address of her still-flourishing establishment at Number 333 MacTavish Place.'

'Thank you, Professor Armbruster.' Holmes rose and shook him by the hand. I extended mine as well, but instead of accepting it he glared at me with malice in his eyes.

'I would advise you to steer clear of people's overcoats in the future,' said he. He turned his attention back to Holmes, who had grasped the doorknob. 'Mind that door; it sticks.'

'So I observed.'

We were on our way down when Holmes stopped upon the staircase landing.

'Watson,' said he, 'would you pardon me whilst I speak with the professor a moment longer? I have forgotten something. There's a good fellow.' He turned and walked briskly back down the corridor.

I sat down on the top step and lit a cigar. It was two thirds gone by the time Holmes returned, wearing an expression which I can only describe as smug. All the way downstairs and across the University grounds he did not say a word. Near the medical library he hailed a hansom, and, as we climbed aboard:

'Number 333 MacTavish Place, driver, and take your time. Those ladies need their sleep.'

Fourteen

No. 333 Mactavish Place

Our driver, who appeared to be familiar with the area, lost no time in conveying us to a seamy neighbourhood buried amidst the maze of ancient and modern structures which typified Scotland's capital city. Here, where grey buildings rolled past in drab succession, each of which appeared to be more tightly shut against the invasion of daylight than the one before, there was little doubt as to what went on beyond their locked doors when the sun was down and the gas lamps were burning. From behind some of them, lines strung with freshly-laundered unmentionables fluttered ostentatiously into view from time to time in the stiff breeze, brazen advertisements of the pleasures awaiting within. We stopped finally before a towering Gothic structure which had once been a fine private dwelling but which had long since deteriorated into a hovel to match its neighbours; over its arched doorway the number 333 was cut into weathered stone.

'A trifle early, ain't you, men?' asked the hefty Scot in the driver's seat, leering, as Holmes paid him. 'They don't open their doors here till after eight.'

'Since you appear to know so much about it, perhaps you would be kind enough to introduce us to the tenants,' responded the detective blandly.

The driver growled a reply which was unintelligible, gave his reins a flip, and lurched off down the street.

The appearance of a cab in that neighbourhood at that hour was apparently unusual enough to warrant inspection, as here and there I spotted blinds being pulled aside in windows on both sides of the street. I tugged my hat down low over my eyes and turned up my coat collar as we headed up the walk towards the front door of No. 333. Holmes chuckled softly.

'You needn't worry about being recognised this far from home, Watson,' said he. 'Even if you were, the observers might find it difficult to explain what business they themselves had in this quarter. Besides, you are drawing more attention to yourself by acting furtive.' He rapped upon the door with the brass knocker which hung in its centre.

There was a long wait, after which we heard footsteps approaching and the door opened a crack to reveal a handsome brown eye and little else. It looked each of us up and down in turn before a husky feminine voice informed us that the establishment was closed.

Holmes removed his hat and introduced us both – to my distress. 'We wish to speak with Miss Fanny Flanagan,' he continued. 'Is the lady still in residence?'

A lengthy silence ensued, during which suspicion glittered in the single exposed eye. Then: 'There is no-one here by that name.' The door began to close.

'It has to do with Henry Jekyll, Miss Flanagan,' said Holmes hastily.

The door stopped. A new glint came into the eye, one of curiosity.

'How did you know?' asked the voice.

'Dialects are a specialty of mine, Miss Flanagan. Thirty years in

Scotland have failed to completely eradicate your stubborn Irish brogue.'

'You are from the police?'

'No, Dr. Watson and I are acting on behalf of a client.'

'Henry Jekyll?'

'It is rather involved. May we come inside?'

There was another long pause. Finally the door was opened fully and we stepped across the threshold. I took off my hat and stared in wonder at our surroundings.

The homeliness of the building's exterior had not prepared me for the splendour within. The floor was concealed beneath a luxurious carpet which was deep enough to tickle my ankles, whilst the walls were half-panelled in very old oak and decorated with fine oils in intricate gilt frames; these details, however, served only to heighten the effect created by the costly wing-backed armchairs of stuffed leather and velvet and the darkly-gleaming curve-legged tables and glass-fronted cabinets stocked with china and delicate *objets d'art* with which the room was furnished. Towards the rear, a graceful old staircase carpeted in deep purple and glittering gold swept upwards to the first floor in the company of colourful tapestries, dark with age, which lined the wall along its far side. It was a home fit, if not for a king, then at least for a prime minister.

But it was our hostess who completed this picture of grace and luxury. Far from the sin-wasted slattern I had expected, Fanny Flanagan was a statuesque woman attired in a flowing dressing-gown of a deep blue material which shimmered as she closed the door and turned to face us, offering us as she did so just a glimpse of a tiny foot shod in pale blue satin beneath the hem. Although my knowledge of her past placed her at middle age, there was nothing either in the fine line of her neck or the smoothly-moulded surface of her oval face to suggest matronliness; indeed, were it not for a single wisp of silver glistening amidst the waves in her auburn hair – which tumbled unfettered about her shoulders

– I should not have guessed her to be beyond five-and-thirty. Aside from that, the years had left their mark only in a set of most appealing laughter-lines which crinkled at the corners of her eyes when she favoured us with her hostess's smile. If like others in her profession she was in the habit of painting her face, such was not evident.

After she had relieved us of our hats and coats and hung them beside the door, she waved us into two of the handsome armchairs with a graceful gesture of her slender right hand. 'Shall I pour you each a glass of brandy?' She stepped towards a table upon which stood an ornate decanter and some glasses.

'Thank you, it is a bit early in the day for us,' said Holmes. I concurred.

She laughed, a merry tinkling sound far back in her throat. 'Of course. I'm sorry. It is force of habit.' She glanced upwards. 'Back to bed, girls; everything is under control.'

I had been uncomfortably aware for some time of a bevy of beautiful young women, who, clad only in flimsy nightdresses, were watching us from the staircase landing. One, a diminutive blonde, appeared to be showing more than passing interest in me. At their mistress's benevolent but firm command, they giggled and fled down the first-floor passageway, naked feet padding on bare wood. Within moments, however, most of them had crept back – notably the blonde, who was now most assuredly studying me from behind the bannister. I squirmed in my seat and wished that I had not been so quick to decline Miss Flanagan's offer of brandy.

'You have a lovely home,' commented Holmes.

'Thank you. It would be a good deal less lavish but for the University. Many of the students find my girls a welcome change from lectures and studying. But you have not come to discuss my *décor*.' She lowered herself gracefully into a straight-backed chair with a bright window behind it – a common practice, I had learnt, amongst women who were unsure of their appearance. In her case the maneuver was unnecessary.

Holmes sketched for her benefit a brief outline of the events which had led us to her parlour, beginning with the Carew murder and finishing with the tale which Professor Armbruster had recounted. At this point she smiled.

'Old 'Brucie,' she mused. 'The students speak of him often.'

'With good reason,' said Holmes. 'Although he is rather less than lucid in some areas – assuming, that is, that Watson did not, as he maintains, run the old gentleman's overcoat up the flagpole in '73' – here he glanced slyly in my direction – 'he experienced no difficulty whatsoever in recalling the incident which cost Jekyll a year of penance when we asked him for any aberration in his former student's past.'

'And you believe that this tale is the source of Henry's present difficulties?'

'I neither believe nor disregard anything until all of the facts are in. However, it is a fundamental tenet of botany that a sudden alteration in the growth of a tree may find its origin in its early development.'

'But it was such a little thing. I hardly remember it myself.'

'An incident which no-one remembers is an incident which is easily distorted. Put your memory to work. What happened that night?'

She shrugged, a delightful little movement involving only one shoulder. 'Come now, Mr. Holmes; you appear to me to be a man of the world. What do you imagine happened?'

'What I imagine, madam, is entirely beside the point. I should like to hear the details in your own words.' His grey eyes flashed fire.

The retort, swift as a rapier thrust, caught our hostess off her guard. She fidgeted beneath Holmes's glare, dropped her eyes; then, defiantly, she met his gaze head-on. Her strength of will was remarkable to behold. 'Nothing happened that night, Mr. Holmes.' Her tone was firm.

'Nothing?' It was the detective's turn to be taken aback.

'Nothing.' She made a tiny gesture of dismissal. 'The boy was drunk. I was working the public-house that night – in those days we were expected to go out and fetch our customers instead of waiting for them to seek us out; Mrs. McGregor was in charge then, the old harridan – anyway, I caught his eye whilst he was drinking with his friends and he lurched over to where I was standing. You should have seen me in those days, Mr. Holmes. I was just sixteen, and a bonny little thing. He wasn't so drunk he missed that. He made a proposition and I accepted it. *Clarice!'*

The tiny blonde had sneaked downstairs without her mistress's knowledge and stretched out a hand from behind my chair to touch my arm. At Miss Flanagan's cry she drew back in fear and remorse and shot back up the stairs like a bullet. A moment later I heard a door slam on the floor above.

'I apologise for Clarice's bad manners, Doctor,' said our hostess, smiling in a strained fashion. 'She is young enough to imagine that she may fall in love in this profession and yet not be hurt. She has much to learn.'

Somehow I received the impression that it was not Clarice at whom her anger was directed, but at me, or rather at the gender to which I belonged. I responded that no apologies were necessary.

'Pray continue, Miss Flanagan,' said Holmes impatiently.

'Where was I?'

'Jekyll made a proposition and you accepted.'

'Yes, of course. You must understand that he was not new to the public-house and that stories concerning his family's wealth were widespread. Moreover, he was very handsome and his manners were impeccable, even in his unsteady condition. These three qualities made the prospect of landing him a matter of some competition; that he chose me from amongst all the girls present flattered me beyond words. As was customary, I obtained the money in advance – it was five bob in those days – and he accompanied me across the street to this house.'

She stopped.

'And then?' pressed the detective.

Again she shrugged. 'Nothing. When he got to my room he fell asleep.'

A silence descended whilst Holmes and I pondered this incredible revelation. At this point the comical side of what had started out as a sordid tale of scandal asserted itself, and we both roared with laughter.

'It strikes you funny now, but I can assure you that it was no laughing matter at the time,' said she with some heat. 'I was young, inexperienced, and deathly afraid of Mrs. McGregor. Rather than tell her what had happened and become the target of her ridicule, I stayed up all night in a chair because there was no room beside that snoring young popinjay on my bed, sprawled as he was across it. The next morning, when everyone was asleep, I succeeded in rousing him – he was still quite unsteady – and helped him downstairs and into a cab. I thought that would be the end of it, but the driver, a nasty sort, said that he would not exert himself getting the young man back to his rooms and refused to take him unless I went along to perform that function. I had no choice but to act as his escort. It cost me four bob for a cab fare there and back.' She shook her head. 'No, Mr. Holmes and Dr. Watson, I reiterate that I felt no desire to laugh.'

'That was the only time you ever saw him?'

'As far as I know he was never seen in this quarter after that.'

'And yet a little while ago you referred to him by his Christian name.'

She smiled faintly, her good humour having in some measure returned. 'I am hardly likely to have forgot the name of my partner in that *débâcle*. I think that you will agree that Dr. Jekyll sounds rather stilted, under the circumstances.'

'I cannot disagree. That, then, is the entire incident as you recollect it?'

'Yes-s-s,' she said, but without conviction. Holmes seized upon it.

'There is something else?'

'It is such a trifle.'

'Great things are naught but a compedium of trifles. Proceed.'

'He muttered in his sleep. His words were so strange that I fancy I can recall them yet.' She passed a slim white hand across her forehead as though to clear away the mist of years.

'"Jekyll the Builder and Jekyll the Carouser," said he. "If I could but separate them, what worlds would be mine!" That was it. He said it again and again. The words varied, but the meaning, if meaning there was, remained the same. Can you make anything of it at all?'

'It seems to have been a pet subject with him,' said Holmes. He sat there a moment longer, brooding. Then he got up. 'I am grateful, Miss Flanagan. If there is any way in which I can return the favour –'

'There is one way.' She rose. 'Please wait.' She lifted her skirts and hurried into the next room amidst rustling satin, leaving us alone in the parlour. The young women gathered at the top of the stairs took advantage of their mistress's absence to converse amongst themselves in low whispers, punctuated at intervals by girlish giggles. I pretended to interest myself in the details of a pastoral landscape which hung upon the opposite wall and tried not to eavesdrop. Holmes appeared to be lost in a world all his own.

The proprietress of the establishment returned shortly, carrying something in a clenched fist. This she pushed into Holmes's open hand as she approached him.

'I would appreciate it if you would give that to Henry Jekyll the next time you see him,' she said. 'I do not relish the idea of owing anybody anything.'

The detective looked down at the bright new shilling which glittered in the palm of his hand, and smiled.

'Consider it done, Madame,' said he.

Fifteen

A CRY FOR HELP?

We had crossed three streets after leaving Fanny Flanagan's house of ill fame before it occurred to me that we were circling back in the direction from which we had come. I began to remark upon this strange behaviour, only to be cut off in mid-sentence when my companion placed a discreet finger to his lips.

'It is as I thought,' he observed in a low murmur after we had progressed a few more steps. 'Do not turn round, but we are being followed. Don't, I say!'

Involuntarily I had turned to look over my shoulder but checked the movement upon his stern command. Behind us I heard stealthy footsteps rounding the corner.

'Who is it?' I whispered.

'I caught a glimpse of him back there when I stopped to light my pipe. I've never seen him before. Keep walking.'

We continued as far as the next corner, where a solitary cab was approaching at a swift pace, its driver evidently in a hurry to be quit of the place after dropping off some late fare from the evening before.

Holmes hailed it.

'He approaches,' warned the detective as we were about to board. 'Be ready for anything.'

'I say, lads, that's my cab.'

Holmes and I turned. The appearance of the newcomer, and the tone in which his statement had been delivered, moved me to squeeze the revolver in my right-hand pocket. He was a brawny Scotsman from the lower classes, attired in a worn ulster from the frayed sleeves of which protruded no cuff of any kind, and a soft, soiled cap whose creased peak all but hid his unshaven features from view, pulled low as it was over his bloodshot left eye. One of his hands was concealed ominously among the folds of his greatcoat.

'I beg your pardon?' said Holmes.

'Don't beg my nothing, laddie. I saw her first and she's mine. Unless you want to settle it the man's way.' Here he leered, showing two rows of tobacco-stained teeth among which many gaps were visible.

Holmes pretended to ignore him and turned to mount the cab. The Scot moved suddenly and something flashed in the hand which he had been hiding.

'Holmes! Look out!' I tried to claw the revolver out of my pocket. The steel sight caught on the cloth, tearing it.

But the detective was ready for him. No sooner did the man lunge forward, thrusting with the knife, than Holmes grasped his outstretched wrist in both hands, crouched, and with the aid of his assailant's own momentum tossed him over his back so that he landed with a jarring thud in the gutter almost beneath the hooves of the cabby's horse. The animal whinnied and tried to rear, but its master had a firm hand on the reins. Taking advantage of that situation, the cabby steered around the man sprawled in the street, unfurled his whip, and left at a brisk trot.

The instant the Scot struck the ground, Holmes, still gripping his wrist, stepped over him and placed the heel of his boot against the back of the man's neck. He then leant forward, twisting the arm as he did so. The knife clattered to the pavement. Nevertheless he maintained pressure on the strained limb. The man on the ground groaned.

'The time has come for answers, my friend,' said Holmes. 'Who are you and why did you try to kill me?'

There was no answer. He increased the pressure. The Scot gasped.

'I wasn't trying to kill no-one!' he blurted.

'In that case, friend, you have much to learn about meeting people. Answer the question!' He twisted harder. The Scot cursed through his teeth.

'As God is my witness, it wasn't your life I was after!' The words came tumbling out all in a breath.

'What, then?' Holmes let up slightly.

'It was supposed to be a warning. Just a warning, nothing more.'

'From whom?'

'I don't know.' Holmes twisted. He gasped. 'I swear it, he never told me his name.' Again the pressure was released. He sighed. 'Have a heart, mate,' he pleaded. 'A man can't hardly collect his thoughts in this state.'

Reluctantly, Holmes let go of the man's arm and stood back to allow him to sit up. He did so slowly and sat there working his abused arm and wincing.

'My name's Ian MacTeague,' he began, 'and you'd know it if you'd spent much time in any theatre in Glasgow or Aberdeen eleven years ago. I've a knife-throwing act like none other in the realm, or at least I did until the girl I used made a wrong move, but that's all in the Assizes records if you care to check it out. Since they let me go I've been making my way in every pub between here and the border, puncturing handkerchiefs and playing-cards at twenty feet for a bob a throw.

'I met him last night in the Piper's. A little fellow he was, scarce came to my collar on tippy-toe. Big head, narrow face, as evil an eye as any I've seen. Fair give me the willies, he did. I'd just bought supper with a hit square through the middle of the ace of trouble. He pulls me into a corner booth and offers me twenty quid if I'd do something for him.

'"Twenty quid!" says I. "Who's to be nobbled, then?"

'"There's no nobbling involved," says he. "At least, not the kind you think. It's to be a warning."

'"Of what sort?"

'"A carve job."

'"What kind of carve job?" says I.

'"As pretty a block letter 'H' as an artist like yourself can manage upon another man's cheek," says he.'

'Good Lord!' I ejaculated.

'How long have you been following us?' Holmes asked.

'Just since this morning. This was the first chance I had to catch you without too many witnesses around.'

'What were your instructions regarding Watson?'

'I was told not to worry about him, as he is merely a buffoon you keep around for your own amusement.'

Holmes snorted. 'My advice to you is that you heed not the advice of others. That "buffoon," as you call him, nearly blew your head off.'

As he spoke, Holmes inclined his chin towards the revolver in my hand, which I had finally succeeded in bringing to light at the expense of my pocket lining. I felt little pride in the compliment, however, as I knew only too well that had the situation been in my hands my friend would be lying in the gutter now occupied by Ian MacTeague with a bloody initial carved upon his cheek.

'Did this fellow mention where he was staying?' Holmes asked the Scot.

MacTeague gave him the name of a hotel I knew well. 'I was to go there and collect a bonus if I had accomplished my objective by this afternoon,' he said. He paused. 'I suppose that now I am to be turned over to the police.'

'Is there any reason why you should not?'

He made no answer. Holmes sighed.

'I am probably committing a grave error,' he said. He signalled for the Scot to climb to his feet. Awkwardly he obeyed, eyeing longingly the knife on the pavement.

'Oh, no, my friend.' Placing a heel on the weapon's wicked blade, the detective reached down, took hold of the haft, and with a sudden exertion snapped it off at the hilt. He then threw both halves into the filth in the gutter. 'If you've the common sense that lies almost invariably beneath the pretensions of the born theatrical performer,' he told the crestfallen knife thrower, 'you'll understand why I did that and won't bother to replace it. There are honest means by which a man may make his way in this world provided that he's up to the task. Watson, we are due elsewhere.'

The hotel to which we had been directed had once catered to an elegant trade, but the march of time and changing tastes had deteriorated both its accoutrements and its clientele, so that the fine old brass fixtures in the lobby had been allowed to turn a brackish green and thin spots marred the nap in the faded burgundy of the carpet. Still, it retained something of its former pride, manifest in the frosty manner of the well-dressed old man behind the desk when Holmes enquired about a guest named Edward Hyde.

'There is no-one by that name staying at this hotel,' he said after consulting the register. Gaunt almost to the point of transparency, his frame spoke of many meals missed in order that he might afford the fine clothes he wore. Rimless spectacles rode high astride his thin, bluish nose, through the lenses of which he managed to give the impression of looking down upon my companion, though in height he was at least two inches the detective's inferior.

'He won't be registered under that name,' Holmes explained, and proceeded to describe our quarry in detail. Recognition glimmered in the clerk's watery eyes.

'His name is Emil Cache,' broke in the latter, before Holmes had finished. 'He checked out two hours ago.'

'May we see his room?'

'If you'd like, but it's been cleaned since his departure.'

The other made a sound of disgust and turned away. 'He's done it again, Watson,' said he when we were back on the street. 'Slipped in and out beneath our very noses. What's more, he is laughing at us.'

'What makes you think that?'

'*Cache* is merely the French for "hide." If that isn't rubbing our noses in it I don't know what is. He's a cunning beast, I'll give him that. No small talent is involved in sneaking past the dozens of official eyes under whose scrutiny one must pass when crossing the border. I know, because I've done it myself.'

'Where do you suppose he's headed?'

'Without doubt, back to London. Even a creature as wily as he cannot hope to finesse his way off the island, wanted as he is, and all game returns to the territory it knows best. This one fled back to his burrow as soon as he was assured his message would be delivered.'

I shuddered at the memory of what MacTeague had told us. 'The man's inhuman! To think that he would have you branded as the Americans do their cattle. He must be terribly afraid that we will learn his awful secret, whatever it is.'

'Afraid? Hardly. Not Hyde.'

'Then what did he hope to gain by having you disfigured?'

'Upon the surface, triumph. Our knowledge of his character certainly does not preclude a capacity for sadism. Upon a deeper level...' He fell silent, his brow knitted in thought.

'What?' said I.

'I am not sure.' Something in his expression told me that what he had said was not just a figure of speech. To this day I can count upon the fingers of one hand the times that Sherlock Holmes has appeared uncertain of his ground, and this was one of them. 'Can it be,' he said at length, 'that after all this time we still do not know him? Can it be that beneath that wicked exterior, thick though it is, there is a desperate soul crying for help? I wonder.' And with that he fell into one of those moody silences from which it was impossible for anyone upon this earth to extricate him.

Sixteen

A New Trail

'We have cleared up one mystery, at any rate,' said I as the familiar duns and greys of London rumbled past our cab window on the way home from King's Cross Station some days later.

It was the latest in a series of half-hearted attempts I had made to rouse Holmes from the grim reverie into which he had descended upon our emergence from the hotel in Edinburgh. For days his speech had been limited to monosyllables when he chose to speak at all, which was seldom, and then only when silence became inconvenient. The parcels which lay unopened upon the seat between us were further examples of how deeply he was involved in this case; normally an omnivorous reader with an insatiable appetite for learning, he had not even bothered to glance at the numerous books which he had acquired in the course of his many visits to the Edinburgh bookstalls. He had, in fact, done little more than recharge and re-light his oily briar again and again during the entire trip across the isle.

'Indeed?' said he, removing the stem from between his teeth for the first time in over an hour. 'And what mystery have we cleared up?'

'Why, the source of the power which Edward Hyde exerts over Dr. Jekyll, of course. The villain is blackmailing him by threatening to expose his thirty-year-old indiscretion with Fanny Flanagan.'

'I rather doubt it.'

'Why?'

'I said before that Universities are hotbeds of gossip. We have in addition the professor's statement that Jekyll's indiscretion was a matter of common knowledge within hours. Even today there must be at least a dozen people who remember the incident. The profit – and the danger – in blackmailing someone lies in the blackmailer's being in sole possession of the damaging details. Why should Jekyll bow to Hyde's will when there are others just as capable of ruining him? Once he has been paid off there is always the danger that the others will follow his lead. Better to bring the whole thing out into the open and brave the consequences. If, that is, there are any, which presupposes that the incident is shocking enough to reverse the effect of the many noble deeds which the doctor has performed in the course of his public life. Besides, Hyde has no evidence with which to back up his claim. No, Watson, the theory no longer holds water. Henry Jekyll is not being held up over the Flanagan affair.'

'Over what, then?'

'Over nothing.'

'I do not understand. How may one man blackmail another over nothing?'

'Obviously, he cannot.'

With that enigmatic statement, he leant his head out of the window and gave the cabby an address which I did not catch. Then he settled back into the seat with a sigh of satisfaction. 'You are not too exhausted, I trust, Watson? I have directed the driver to make a brief stopover at Jekyll's residence.'

'Please, Holmes, one confusion at a time.' At that moment I could cheerfully have strangled him but succeeded in controlling myself with an effort. 'Explain how Hyde has managed to make Jekyll dance to his tune with nothing to back him up.'

'A difficult equation, is it not? And yet it becomes so much simpler once we remove the blackmail theory.'

'No blackmail?'

'None whatsoever. Has it not occurred to you that a man may have other reasons for jeopardising his career and his reputation in order to protect an acquaintance?'

'I can think of none.'

'Of course you can. If, for example, you were to pick up tomorrow's edition of the *Times* and read that your friend Sherlock Holmes was being sought for murder, what action would you take?'

'I would of course make use of every resource I had to clear you of the charge. But what —'

'Precisely! And I in turn would do the same for you if you were ever to find yourself in that unlikely position. What do you suppose would be our motive for behaving in this manner?'

'The conviction that the other is innocent.'

'That goes without saying. But would there be no other reason? Something less tangible, perhaps?'

'Why, friendship!'

'Bravo!' He applauded silently.

'But the situations are vastly different,' I protested. 'I can think of no two people who are less suited for friendship than Henry Jekyll and Edward Hyde. The pair are like night and day.'

'Who are we to question the intricacies of attraction? I dare say that had someone informed you five years ago that you, a physician on a pension from the British Army, would soon be sharing lodgings with a man who has been known to practise his marksmanship indoors and to beat the cadavers in a dissecting-room with a truncheon in order to determine to what extent the body may be bruised after death, you would have denounced him as a madman. Opposites attract, Watson; surely you remember that from your scientific training. But here we are already. I advise you henceforth to look formidable and to let me do the talking.'

I had no time to enquire into his meaning, for at that moment he bounded to the kerb in front of Jekyll's elegant home, directed the driver to wait, and strode up the flagstone walk to the front door.

Poole, the elderly butler, answered his knock in a trice.

'We wish to see your master upon a matter of extreme importance,' snapped Holmes in a tone which brooked no protest.

'I am sorry, sir, but that is impossible.' The manservant's voice was cool. He appeared to recognise us, though it had been well over a year since our only meeting. 'Dr. Jekyll is indisposed and cannot receive visitors. Perhaps you would care to leave a message?'

'The time for playing the dutiful domestic is past, Poole. I have reason to believe that Edward Hyde, the Westminster murderer, is concealed beneath this roof. If you do not let us in I shall summon the police and they will be here by nightfall with a warrant to search the premises. Which shall it be?'

For a space the two stared at each other, the butler's eyes of washed-out blue fixed upon the grey fire of my companion's. The former wavered and their owner appeared about to give in when they altered their focus suddenly to something beyond Holmes's shoulder and relief swept his withered features.

'I believe that these gentlemen are leaving, Bradshaw,' said he. 'You may escort them to their cab.'

We turned. Bradshaw was an enormous man whose footman's livery barely contained the bulging muscles of his arms and chest. From his spotless white collar sprouted a neck and head like those of a bull, with a broad blank face and innocent-looking eyes spread wide beneath sandy blond hair cut in bangs over his forehead. He towered over Holmes by several inches. Responding to the butler's command, he stepped forward to escort us in what was probably the only way he knew, his arms bowed in the fashion of a wrestler advancing towards his opponent.

Holmes struck his boxer's stance and let fly with a resounding right cross to the big man's jaw. Bradshaw's head turned a fraction of an inch. The detective's eyes widened ever so slightly at this evidence of his impotence.

'Let us go, Watson,' said he, grasping my wrist and ducking beneath the footman's outstretched left arm.

As we returned to the cab I glanced back towards the top of the steps, where Poole and the hulking Bradshaw stood watching us. It struck me that, for the professed gentility of West End society, the landscape was overrun with sinister servants.

'Round the corner, cabby,' Holmes whispered to the driver. We proceeded as directed, observed all the way by the two men at the front door. Once out of sight, Holmes signalled the cabby to halt.

'When all else fails, go directly to the source,' said my companion as we alighted before the bleak facade of that part of Jekyll's home which faced upon the bystreet.

Again the driver was asked to wait, and as we descended the short flight of steps which led from the street to the door, Holmes drew from a pocket of his coat a slim leather case which I recognised. From it he selected an instrument of shining metal which ended in a flattened point.

'Tell me, Watson,' said he, in a voice scarcely above a whisper, 'have you any reservations concerning unlawful activity when it is directed towards a noble end?'

'I suppose that would depend upon the end,' said I.

'Would you consider justice noble enough?'

'Decidedly.'

'Then be good enough to stand guard whilst I explore the possibilities of this lock.'

I took up a position at the top of the steps whilst he inserted the instrument into the keyhole of the door's ancient lock. It was a stubborn mechanism, and more than once as he struggled with it I heard him curse beneath his breath. At length, however, there was a metallic snap, Holmes uttered a small cry of triumph, and the door was pushed open.

A narrow corridor led us into a large theatre, which, illuminated greyly through a dingy skylight, contained laboratory apparatus and a profusion of opened packing crates heaped with straw upon the flagstones. To our right, a short flight of steps communicated with a red baize door, whilst to our left stood a row of narrow plank doors which appeared to conceal closets. Holmes chose our most promising course and together we climbed the stairs to the red door. Here he placed both of his hands upon the plain knob and turned it carefully, leaning into as he did so. The door moved a fraction of an inch and stopped.

'Bolted.' He hesitated, then rapped sharply upon the door.

'Go away, Poole!' snarled a voice from within. 'I left specific instructions that I was not to be disturbed.'

'This is Sherlock Holmes.' My companion spoke sternly. 'An audience with me now may spare you a visit with the police later.'

There was a long silence. Finally the doctor's heavy tread was heard approaching and the bolt was shot back. The door opened to reveal Henry Jekyll in a white smock.

He had changed little in the fifteen months which had elapsed since our last and only meeting, but he had changed. Creases underscored his crisp blue eyes where before there had only been smoothest skin. The eyes themselves were restless in their socket, as though he expected danger from some quarter but was not sure when it would come or what form it would take when it did. Lines of concern had etched their way from his nostrils to the corners of his wide mouth. The silver at his temples had spread to encompass his widow's-peak, which was itself perceptibly thinner. The changes themselves might not have been noticeable even to his closest friends, but to the trained medical eye everything about him – his appearance, his nervous mannerisms, the agitated way in which he stood – suggested an air of general dissipation. That he had been operating under great strain for some time was self-evident.

In his right hand he held a pair of those metal tongs which I had seen Holmes use many times to lift a test tube filled with steaming liquid from atop his Bunsen burner, and these he waved angrily as he addressed us.

'What is the meaning of this intrusion?' he demanded. 'Explain yourself or, by thunder, I shall be the one who summons the police!'

For all his rage it was evident that he was striving valiantly to hold himself in check. Just why, I did not know. But his entire being shook with the effort.

Holmes presented a calm exterior. 'I rather doubt that you will choose that route, Dr. Jekyll. A cobra does not invite a troupe of mongooses into its den.'

'And just what is that supposed to mean?'

'Oh, very well, if you insist upon carrying through with this charade. I am speaking of Edward Hyde, the accused murdered of Sir Danvers Carew, and the fact that you are harbouring him in your home.'

It may be that the tension of the moment, combined with my own exhaustion after the long journey from Scotland, caused my imagination to soar to ridiculous heights, but it seemed to me that an expression of immense relief swept across the doctor's open features after Holmes had levelled his charge. Whatever it meant, however, it was gone in the next instant, replaced by indignation.

'That is a serious accusation,' said he warningly. 'Were you to repeat it in front of witnesses I should have you up on charges by tomorrow morning.'

'Spare me your rhetoric,' Holmes countered. 'Will you submit to a search of the premises?'

'I most emphatically will not!'

'It is your house, and that is your right. But that will not be sufficient to stop the police when they arrive with a warrant.'

Jekyll's anger altered visibly to consternation. His dynamic eyes took on an introspective look; I could almost see the workings of his magnificent brain. Presently he drew back and flung the door wide.

'I am a busy man,' said he. 'I cannot afford to leave my work whilst a battalion of ill-mannered oafs in uniform snoop about the place, smearing my slides and knocking over my equipment. Conduct your search and be done with it.'

It was a homely little room, an ordinary study but for the presence of numerous scientific paraphernalia. These included a number of glazed presses filled with retorts and test tubes, some of which contained chemicals of varying hues and density, and a powerful microscope beneath which a slide bearing a quantity of white powder was clamped. In the centre of the chamber stood a deal table upon which a glass vessel filled over atop the blue flame of a Bunsen burner. Well-thumbed volumes bound in leather and bearing titles of a chemical nature crowded a pair of tall bookcases along the left wall and formed precarious stacks upon the tables. Some of these were propped open for easy reference. A cheval-glass, curiously out of place in these surroudings, stood in a corner, its polished face turned inexplicably towards the ceiling. A fire crackled in the grate at the far end of the room before which was placed a shabby but comfortable-looking armchair. Upon one arm was balanced a dish containing the remnants of a meal. Three barred windows overlooked a closed court, upon the opposite side of which loomed Jekyll's fine old residence.

Holmes circled the room briskly and returned to our host. 'Thank you, Doctor. I think that we have seen enough.' He stared suddenly at the scientist. 'Dr. Jekyll, are you all right?'

All the blood had drained from the older man's face, leaving it nearly as pale as the smock he was wearing.

'Mother of God!' he cried in a choked voice. 'It is too soon! Too soon after the last time!'

Holmes repeated his query, more urgently.

Jekyll snapped, 'I am quite well. Please leave.' It was a demand as well as a plea. He was shaking visibly.

'Watson is a physician. Perhaps —'

'I am well, I said!' He was shouting now. He seized us each by the shoulder and propelled us with a madman's strength towards the open doorway. 'Get out!' He pushed us outside and slammed the door. The report of the bolt sliding home followed an instant later.

For a moment we stood there, neither of us knowing what action to take, whilst from inside came the sounds of violent convulsions punctuated by breaking glass. Then silence. Holmes rapped tentatively upon the door.

'Dr. Jekyll?'

'Who is it?' The answering voice was harsh, little more than a grating whisper. Holmes appeared taken aback by it.

'It is I, Sherlock Holmes. Are you well?'

'I am all right. Go away!'

'You are certain?'

'Begone, I said!' The roar shook the door panels. Reluctantly we obeyed.

'What do you suppose that was all about?' I asked my companion back in the cab.

'I do not know.' He appeared deep in thought.

'Did you really believe that he was concealing Hyde?'

'Not for one minute. I wished merely to get a look at Jekyll's laboratory and confirm my suspicions. I succeeded in doing both.'

'And?'

'No doubt you wondered what prompted my return to Professor Armbruster's study at the University of Edinburgh,' said he.

I pretended tolerance of this seeming irrelevance by nodding. 'I supposed that you would tell me when you thought it right.'

'Your patience is commendable. I have been convinced for some time that the roots of Jekyll's recent behavior go back to his career at the University. When the blackmail theory evaporated, I decided to concentrate upon his course of study. One can learn much about a man by his interests. With this in mind I asked the professor for Jekyll's reading list during his student days. As I said, the old scholar has a remarkably lucid memory in some areas; he provided me, in short order, with a complete rundown of those titles which occupied most of the young man's time. Many of the works are out of print, and I had the devil of a time tracking them all down. But track them down I did, and here you see the results.' He patted the parcels which lay beside him upon the seat.

'I fail to see what that has to do with this latest confrontation,' said I.

'Many of the works deal with chemistry and science, though I have Armbruster's testimony that none of them was required for the classes which Jekyll attended. A glimpse of the great man's laboratory – a chemical storehouse such as I dream of someday owning myself –

confirmed my belief that he is still engaging in chemical research. I feel certain now that I am on the right track.'

'On the track of what?'

'If I knew that, Watson, I could save myself many weeks of work.' He looked at me then, and his eyes were as bright as twin suns. 'I intend to bury myself in the perusal of those volumes which sent Henry Jekyll upon his current path of destruction. In so doing, I shall follow the trail laid down by a brilliant mind exactly as I would follow that left by a culprit's boots. It is a task well-nigh impossible, for it pre-supposes that I can arrive within these next few weeks at the same conclusion which took Jekyll thirty years to reach. But there is no alternative. Everywhere else lies impasse.'

'And in the meantime?'

'In the meantime a killer will be free to roam the streets. We can but pray that his urge to destroy will remain in check until we have enough to ensure that he will roam them no more.'

Having delivered this statement, he tore the wrapping from one of the parcels – a weighty volume entitled *Wilton's Elements of Chemistry* – and began reading from page one whilst the hansom in which we were riding bucked and rumbled over the cobblestones on the way to Baker Street.

Seventeen

THE MAN IN THE LABORATORY

As is typical for London, the spring of 1885 was heralded by days of cold and bluster which were every bit as severe as anything which the long winter had offered. Icy gales howled down deserted streets, whimpered round chimneys and beneath cornices, cast great handfuls of snow and freezing rain rattling against windowpanes thick with frost. Wisps of greasy brown fog clung to the gas lamps as if holding on lest they be torn asunder by the relentless wind. The streets themselves glistened beneath a sheen of ice, and what little traffic there was made less than snails' progress upon the slick surface. Like almost everyone else in the besieged city, Holmes and I were content to remain prisoners in our own home, engaged in sedentary pursuits and drawing comfort from our own little hearth whilst the elements raged without. The weather was of little consequence, however, as for two months my fellow-lodger had scarcely stirred from his armchair before the fire save to dine and replenish his supply of shag, so engrossed was he in the study of that ponderous stack of reading material which he had brought with him from Edinburgh. He read rapidly, finishing an average of a volume a day, then casting it aside to reach for another from atop the pile. In no time at all the floor round his feet became a litter of discarded books, some of which he returned to on occasion in order to check some point which he either had forgotten or wished to confirm with what he had just read. By the beginning of March our sitting-room had begun to resemble Professor Armbruster's cluttered study.

The extent of his immersion may be measured by the fact that he barely commented when, less than a fortnight after our return from Scotland, Dr. Hastie Lanyon's obituary appeared in all of the newspapers. Death was attributed to 'overwork and a weakened constitution.' His own prediction regarding his life expectancy had come true almost to the day. For Holmes, however, he had become a non-entity the moment he ceased to play a crucial role in the problem upon which we were engaged.

Thus undistracted, I succeeded in putting together a satisfactory first draft of those events which had led to the solution of the Lauriston Gardens mystery and began the laborious process of translating it into acceptable English. I expended several bottles of ink and tossed away something in excess of a ream of foolscap during this stage of the project, much to the chagrin of Mrs. Hudson, whose task it was to empty our trash baskets each morning and afternoon. I confess that Holmes and I were too busy to take much notice of her complaints.

There were times, however, as upon the Ides of March, when even such a sedentary soul as I grew alarmed at my friend's immobility and demanded that he step out and take the air, if only for an hour. Rather than suffer further remonstration, on this particular morning Holmes climbed out from beneath his books and girded himself to face the weather, muttering something about visiting his favourite chemists' shops as he went out the door. I did not see him again for the better part of the day, and when as the supper hour was approaching he re-appeared bearing his new acquisitions wrapped in bundles beneath his arm, he was in such visibly good spirits that I congratulated myself upon the wisdom of my advice, until he told me the reason for his cheer.

'You are aware, Watson, of my observations upon the foolhardy human habit of attempting to reason without sufficient data,' he said as he divested himself of headgear and wrap. 'I am therefore placing myself in an embarrassing position by calling upon you to guess whom I encountered today at Maw & Sons.'

'I cannot think,' said I.

'Our friend Poole.'

'Jekyll's butler! Whatever was he after in a chemist's?'

'Something for his master, without doubt. He was unsuccessful, as Maw informed him in no uncertain terms that Jekyll himself had taken the last of it from his shelf some months ago. I overheard this reply as I was coming in. Poole seemed greatly troubled on his way out and would have walked right on past me had I not called his name. He would not tell me what he was about. Orders from his master, I warrant, though I got the distinct impression that he knew little more about the business than I. I attempted to question Maw after he left, but that worthy gentleman had overheard us and did not deem it advisable to explain the nature of the order. That is of little consequence, however.'

'What do you mean?'

'Ah, you must not ask me that just yet.' He unwrapped his parcels – they contained the usual miscellany of bottles, phials, and packets of substances beyond my ken – and put them away amongst shelves above his chemical table. 'Be satisfied to know that this latest development has a made-to-order place in the theory that I am formulating. All that remains is for me to satisfy myself that such things are possible.' And with that he returned to his studies.

We were not without visitors during this period. I find it recorded in my notebook that we were blessed no fewer than seven times with the presence of Inspector Newcomen of Scotland Yard, and that upon each occasion he had departed in an even blacker humour than that in which he had arrived. The Inspector had gotten it into his head that Holmes was doing nothing to earn whatever fee he was charging the British Empire for his services in the Hyde case (he had, in fact, offered them free of charge), and finding the unofficial detective curled up in an armchair with a book across his knees each time he came to call did little to allay his suspicions. Since a scene was inevitable, I learnt to dread his visits much as an impoverished tenant fears the approaching footsteps of his landlord.

It was the evening of my fellow-tenant's return from Maw & Sons when the Inspector stepped into the house just as Mrs. Hudson had been preparing to retire. She ushered him into our chambers and, after asking us to lock up when our visitor had left, withdrew to her own quarters. Holmes had a short time before flung down a scientific tract which he had finished reading and begun studying a half-century-old edition of *Faust* in the original German. Newcomen shot him a contemptuous glance as he handed me his billycock and shining waterproof.

'I would expect more action from your brother Mycroft,' he sneered. 'I suppose that you are going to tell me that reading some hoary old epic will show you some clue to the whereabouts of Edward Hyde.'

'I will not if you do not wish me to do so,' said Holmes without looking up.

The Inspector slouched into the seat opposite him. 'All right, tell me what you have found.'

'A very interesting passage. It occurs in the Prologue, wherein the Lord speaks to Mephistopheles. I shall attempt to translate: "A good man, through obscurest aspiration, has still an instinct of the one true way".'

'Fascinating.' Newcomen lit a cigar and tossed down the match with a savage gesture. 'Now tell me what it means.'

'Simply defined, it is an expression of the unsinkable nobility of Man.'

'An admirable premise, but what has it to do with tracking down a murderer?'

Holmes shrugged. 'Who can say? Perhaps nothing. Perhaps everything. But I believe that Watson will agree with me that the statement suits a man who is known to both of us.'

'Bah!' The Inspector sprang to his feet and began pacing the room in stiff strides, fists thrust deep in his trouser-pockets. 'All of London lies naked at the feet of a madman and you persist in making up riddles which no-one can answer. More than once you have made reference to this other man, and yet when I ask you who it is you refuse to tell me. If you are withholding evidence in this case I shall see you in the dock, no matter how high your authority.'

'A man's theories are his own, Inspector. I have not divulged mine only because it is as yet untested. Rest assured that when it bears fruit you will be the first to know.'

'How long must I wait? The newspapers are screaming for my badge and the Commissioner is beginning to listen. If something solid does not turn up soon I shall find myself back in uniform, patrolling the blackest alleys in the East End. I beg of you, Mr. Holmes, give me something to go on.' Gone was the bullying symbol of authority of a few moments before, replaced by a supplicant. Desperation shone in his normally cold grey eyes. He chewed the ends of his moustache.

Holmes looked up at him for the first time. His expression was sympathetic. 'That is beyond my power, Inspector.' said he. Newcomen's hopeful face fell in. 'I can, however, give you my word that by the end of this month there will be no more mystery. If we are fortunate, the man whom you seek will be in the hands of justice shortly thereafter. Beyond that I promise nothing.'

'It is a vague promise,' said the other. But there was new hope in his voice.

'It is vague merely because I cannot foretell upcoming events. I have, as I said, formulated a theory which fits all of the facts. I could not have done so but for the aid of these books. But it is a fanciful theory, and I fear that once you learn of it you will think me mad. I have yet to be convinced of it myself. If, however, I am correct, then the solution far exceeds the boundaries of simple domestic crime, and you and I may with some confidence expect to see our names included in the work of some ambitious historian before our span has ended. It may be that we have stumbled onto a stage more vast than any upon which ever we have performed. The very possibilities steal my breath away.'

Newcomen eyed him curiously. 'If I had not heard what I have about you from people whose opinions I respect, I would accuse you of indulging in idle bombast.'

'I have my faults — no-one knows that better than Dr. Watson — but idleness is not amongst them. I waste neither words nor actions.'

'Of the latter I have no doubt' The Inspector snatched his hat and waterproof from the hook upon which they were hung and donned them. 'The end of the month, then,' said he, grasping the doorknob. 'I shall hold you to that.' He went out, slamming the door behind him. I heard his waterproof rustling all the way down the stairs, followed by the bang of the front door. Holmes glanced at the clock upon the mantelpiece, yawned, and leant forward to knock out his pipe upon the grate.

'Bedtime, Watson,' said he, laying aside *Faust.* 'Be good enough to go downstairs and lock up whilst I snatch a few minutes with my Stradivarius. Otherwise I shall dream of Goethe's Hell all night through.' He made a long arm and lifted his violin and bow out of their case.

The strains of something by Liszt followed me as I set about securing the house for the night, and continued as I came back upstairs and then mounted the flight to my own bedroom. By the time I was beneath the counterpane, however, he had exchanged the soaring notes of the Hungarian composer for some eerily beautiful melody which put me in mind of gypsies swaying about a campfire in some lonely moonlit glade. I could not identify it, which may or may not have meant that he was playing some composition of his own. I drifted off with it singing about my ears.

I cannot say how long I had been asleep when I woke to find my friend's spare figure standing over me, but it could not have been too great a time, for it was still dark out and the beam of moonlight which fell upon him from the window had not noticeably shifted its position since my retiring. He was dressed in his Inverness and ear-flapped cap. I came alert all of a sudden, for that taut face and those glistening eyes could mean only one thing. I sat up, blinking.

'Holmes, what is it?'

'There is no time to explain, Watson,' said he. His voice held that strident note which went hand-in-hand with the volcanic action of his brain and body when the *dénouement* was at hand. 'Get up and get dressed if you care to accompany me, whilst I hail us a cab. If I am right there is not a second to be lost.' He turned away without waiting for an answer. 'And bring your revolver!' he shouted on his way downstairs.

Five minutes later we were sharing a hansom on its way east at breakneck speed over the treacherous street surface, rocking and fishtailing as we took the corners.

'Where are we bound this time?' I was forced to shout to make myself heard over the clatter of hooves, and to hold onto my hat with one hand and the side of the conveyance with the other. The air was bitingly cold.

'Jekyll's house,' snapped my companion, now little more than a keen silhouette in the flashing illumination of the racing gas lamps. The cords in his lean neck stood out like piano wire. 'No fool was ever so blind as I have been tonight. I pray that we are not too late.'

For all our haste, as we turned into Jekyll's street we nearly collided with a hansom which was flying in the opposite direction at the same harrowing rate. As it thundered past, the light from the corner gas lamp fell full upon the pale, drawn features of its elderly occupant, in whose anxious expression there was such a singularity of purpose that I doubted he was even aware of the accident which had been so narrowly averted.

'Holmes!' I cried as the cabs separated. 'That was Poole, Jekyll's butler!'

He nodded curtly but said nothing. His countenance was grimmer than ever.

Every light in Jekyll's house was burning when we swung round the corner and came to a bouncing halt on the by-street side. Holmes sprang from the cab.

'It is as I feared, Watson; the worst has happened.' He hastened across the kerb and down the steps to the door which led into the theatre. A tug at the knob confirmed that the door was locked. He cursed. 'I came away without my burglar's kit! I'll need your good shoulder, Watson.'

Together we braced ourselves before the door, strongest shoulders foremost.

'On the count of three,' Holmes directed. 'One, two, three!'

We struck simultaneously. Pain shot through me. The door creaked in its casing; no more.

'Again. One, two, three!'

This time the planks bounced and a noise like a pistol-shot rang out.

Upon examination in the lamplight, it developed that a portion of the wood round the rusted lock had split in a large semi-circular fissure.

'One more time, Watson. One, two, three!'

The door sprang open with a splattering crack and we stumbled into the threatre. Scrambling to maintain our balance, we let our momentum carry us forward down the corridor, where in the gloom I perceived the outline of a vague grey figure standing at the nether end. At our entrance it let out a strangled cry, wheeled, and bounded monkey-fashion up the flight of steps which led to the red baize door of the doctor's laboratory.

'After him!' Holmes cried.

During my ball-playing days at Blackheath I had won the admiration of my teammates for my speed afoot, but Holmes was several strides ahead of me as he took the steps two at a time upon the heels of our quarry and seized the door just as it was being slammed shut. With great effort he succeeded in shouldering his way inside. I entered an instant later, drawing my revolver from the pocket of my coat.

I was right glad that I had done so, for in the light of the gas fixture I found myself face to face with Edward Hyde.

Eighteen

SHOCK!

The reader may dismiss me as shallow, but I confess that in spite of what I know about the man, and independent of that unspeakable revulsion which his very presence engendered, I found his appearance upon this occasion grotesquely comical. For some reason he had seen fit to don the clothing of his benefactor; the sight of his shrunken frame enveloped in Jekyll's voluminous white smock, the doctor's collar hanging loose about his scrawny neck and his boots hidden beneath the folds of trousers which were several sizes too large for him, was so ludicrously like that of a small child playing 'dress-up' with his father's wardrobe that in my hyper-excited state I might have been moved to laughter had it not been for the savage expression upon Hyde's wolfish countenance.

The eyes beneath the soaring brows were wild, the aquiline nostrils flaring. White teeth flashed in a snarl of warning, whilst his razor-edged features, their sharpness intensified in contrast with his massive head, writhed with a hatred deep as Cain's. He hissed like an animal at bay.

He had snatched up a graduated glass from the work-table at his back, in which some evil-looking yellowish liquid boiled and spumed vapour, and now he stood holding it before him as if it were a weapon with which he hoped to keep us at arm's length.

'Meddling imbeciles!' Suddenly I recognised that harsh, croaking whisper as the same voice which we had heard enjoining us to leave during our last visit to the laboratory. But that was impossible, for we had searched the room thoroughly and found no trace of the fiend. It was difficult to think straight in the presence of this malevolent force. 'What right have you to interrupt me in my work?'

An empty retort reposed atop the burning Bunsen upon the table behind him. He had evidently just transferred its contents into the glass in his hand when our labours at the street door had forced him to investigate.

'The right of citizens to apprehend a foul murderer!' said I, raising my revolver.

He was silent for a moment; then, inexplicably, his snarl altered to become an obscene smirk.

'A foul murderer,' he echoed. 'That is a curious appellation for one who has unlocked the secret of a thousand generations. What matter a single life when mankind teeters upon the brink of a discovery which will change for ever the shape of the world in which we live?'

'Do not attempt to confuse us,' I barked. 'We have been on your trail too long to let go now.'

'Let him speak, Watson,' said Holmes.

I glanced at my companion and noticed for the first time that, though he had drawn his own pistol, it was not aimed at Hyde but rather at the floor between his feet.

'But, Holmes!'

Hyde laughed — a mocking sound which turned the blood in my veins to ice.

'Heed your friend's words. He speaks wisdom.' He sneered. 'You with your courage and your honour. Hypocrisy! That at least is one crime with which you cannot charge me. My nature is plain for all to see.'

'Wickedness!'

'Wickedness – by your standards. But you sail beneath false colours. I, however, am exactly what you see; no more and no less. Edward Hyde, whom you can trust not to be worthy of your trust. Now, Doctor, which of us is the more honest?'

'You speak in riddles! What have you done with Jekyll?'

He ignored the question and addressed himself to Holmes. 'The fact that you are here on this most fateful of nights indicates that you suspect the truth. Is that so?'

'I suspected it nearly two months ago, when I heard your voice behind this door,' Holmes informed him. 'I did not become convinced of it until tonight.'

Hyde's reaction was a mixture of astonishment and fascination. After a pause he said, 'I imagined that Jekyll was the only man capable of comprehending such an idea. And he was able to do so only after three decades of study. Is it that he is dense or that you are that brilliant?'

'Neither. It is the trail-blazer who assumes all the risks and paves the way for them to follow. Jekyll's studies and the evidence of recent months led me to this conclusion.'

'You do yourself an injustice.'

'On the contrary, it is you who have suffered the most harm through your own actions.'

Hyde considered that. At length he nodded, dipping his great head down and then up in the fashion of a huge reptile. In his eyes I perceived an unfathomable sorrow which was hardly in keeping with his image.

'I am certain that Jekyll would concur.'

'Hold on!' I cried. 'I realise that I am a poor simpleton, but this entire conversation is beyond me. Where is Jekyll?'

Hyde's attention remained centred upon Holmes. 'He does not know?'

Holmes shook his head.

'A fair question, Doctor.' The murderer turned his eyes upon me, and now there was no trace in them of anything but loathsome arrogance. My flesh crawled; I had all I could do to restrain myself from squeezing the trigger of my weapon and removing this malignant growth from the face of the earth. He continued. 'To answer it would take too many words and consume valuable time, time which I no longer have. How is your health?'

The question caught me off-guard. 'Good,' I blurted out, without thinking. 'Excellent.'

'For your sake I hope that you speak the truth. What you are about to see sent Hastie Lanyon to an early grave. Behold!' He raised the foaming glass to his lips and downed the bilious liquid in a single draught.

The reaction was immediate and startling. The glass shattered at his feet; he reeled backwards, clutching at the edge of the table for support. His face turned purple and he doubled over. Gasping and strangling noises issued from his throat.

'He's poisoned himself!' I cried, and started forward. Holmes's iron grip closed about my right arm. I stopped.

Hyde was bent with his face inches from the plank floor, arms folded about his torso, hugging himself. He was panting. Perspiration streamed down his face and dripped from his chin to the floor. His features writhed. He appeared to be going through his final agonies.

And then a curious thing began to happen.

Slowly he came up from his crouch, and as he did so his body seemed to swell and his contorted features to slacken. As do the pockets of a silken bag when it takes on gas, the folds and wrinkles in his ill-fitting attire appeared to straighten and fill. Hyde's ape-like crest of hair fell forward over his brow and, incredibly, began to soften and change colour. Before my eyes it turned from raven black to silver-streaked chestnut. His features broadened; his shrunken body grew into proportion with his oversize head. Gradually his breathing returned to normal.

And there, in the spot where seconds before Edward Hyde had stood, a dissipated Henry Jekyll raised his head and met our astonished gazes with steady blue eyes.

Nineteen

DR. JEKYLL AND MR. HYDE

I felt the blood rush from my face as though a valve had suddenly been thrown open somewhere in my system. My knees turned to water and I clutched at the door for support. The revolver I was holding fell with a thud to the floor. I made no attempt to retrieve it.

Out of the corner of my eye I glimpsed a pale and shaken Sherlock Holmes, and thus received a mirror-view of myself at that moment. Though it was obvious that he had known what was coming, the naked fact of its happening in his presence was quite another thing. His jaw fell open slightly and his eyes started from their sockets, reactions which in him were the equivalent of a normal man's fit of hysterics.

Henry Jekyll ran a quivering hand through his dishevelled hair. He swayed unsteadily, but aside from these outward signs he showed no ill effects from the drug which had wrought such an earth-shattering result. He smiled weakly and without mirth.

'I would be grateful it you would bolt the door behind you,' said he in a drained voice. 'My butler is missing and I fear that he will not return alone.' When, in response to Holmes's nod, I had done as requested, the scientist turned and walked unsteadily over to where a cheery fire crackled in the grate. There he collapsed into his worn armchair as if his legs had suddenly been kicked from beneath him.

'Please sit down. I suppose that I owe you an explanation, but I suspect that my time is short. Soon Henry Jekyll will vanish from the face of the earth and no power this side of Heaven or Hell will bring him back.'

A straight-backed wooden chair stood on either side of the fire. I selected one and sank down onto it. Holmes remained standing, his back to the fire. Almost unconsciously he drew his black briar from the pocket of his waistcoat, filled it, and lit it with a coal from the grate. Outwardly at least, he had regained his calm demeanour.

'You may begin at the beginning, Doctor.'

Jekyll made a gesture of dismissal. 'That won't be necessary. It's evident that you are familiar with my observations upon that imperfect species which we call the human race. That two men, one noble, the other base, exist side by side in each of our bodies became an obsession with me whilst I was attending the University. I was convinced that my true calling lay in dedicating my life towards eradicating that cruder self which has led to the undoing of so many honourable men. To accomplish that, it was first necessary that the two be separated. By graduation I had already determined that such a separation was chemically possible; it remained only for me to narrow down the proper elements. Since the combinations were nearly limitless, I was fully aware that I might die long before I had attained my goal. By that time, though, I hoped to have found a successor who would be willing to take up where I had left off. Towards this end I endeavoured to enlist my friend Lanyon, only to have him condemn my theories as "unscientific balderdash" when I laid them before him. From that moment dates the rift between us which interested you early in your investigation.

'Lest I begin to sound like a martyr, I must confess that my motives were not entirely altruistic. Born into a wealthy, respectable family, I had all my life been warned that there were certain things which a Jekyll must not do, or risk compromising the family honour. Being that imperfect combination of opposing wills, I longed as a result to taste of some of the pleasures which were forbidden me. The first step – separating the noble member from the base – might release my other self to sample those distractions without jeopardy. A scandal which took place during my student days because of this longing, far from dissuading me, bolstered my determination to continue and thus realise this first goal. Afterwards, I promised myself, I would press onwards until my worthier work was done. How foolish we are in our youth!

'The breakthrough came something over two years ago. A certain white powder – it shall remain nameless – when mixed with the solution which I had long ago decided upon as the correct one, had the catalytic effect which I sought. I drank it, with the results which you have yourselves just witnessed, though in reverse. I have dealt in detail with my first experiences under the drug's effects in my written confession addressed to Utterson and lying unfinished upon yonder table. I wish that I could convey something of the freedom which I felt in my new self. The creature whom I was to christen Edward Hyde was young and thoroughly unfettered by the chains of conscience. Unlike the rest of us, he was a perfect being, but only in that his wickedness was pure and unadulterated. Hypocrisy was not in his nature, for his foulest thoughts were written plainly upon his face. This was the reason for that seemingly unfounded loathing with which everyone who encountered him was stricken.

'It is painful for me to admit that there my experiments halted. The temptation to turn this freedom to my own advantage was too great, and once, after an embarrassing episode in which Jekyll was forced to compensate the family of a young girl for a wrong which Hyde had done her, I had established Hyde's independence with a banking-account of his own and a home in Soho, I dedicated myself body and soul to a double life. By day Henry Jekyll donated his services to the betterment of mankind; by night Edward Hyde did his level best to undo that good. For a period we cancelled each other out.

'My first inkling of danger came some months later when my other self appeared without the aid of the drug. I had gone to sleep as Henry Jekyll and had awakened as Edward Hyde. It required a double dose of the powder upon that occasion to return me to my normal state.

'It was a frightening development, for it meant that the character of Hyde had begun to dominate that of Jekyll. If the situation were allowed to continue, I reasoned, it was only a matter of time before Hyde became the natural personality, whilst Jekyll was reduced to the aberration. It was possible, in fact, that things would reach the point where the elderly and respected doctor would vanish entirely from existence. I prepared for the worst and drew up that will which caused Utterson so much consternation and eventually brought you into the picture, in which I stipulated that, in the event of the death or disappearance of Dr. Jekyll, all of his possessions would pass into the hands of his good friend Mr. Hyde. It is evidence of my selfishness that I feared to cast my other self adrift with neither finances nor shelter.

'At the same time, I took steps to see that the worst did not happen, and for a period of two months abstained from drinking my unholy brew. Had I been stronger, I would have destroyed my notes, dumped out my chemicals, and been a happy man today. I was fool enough, however, and weak enough, to believe that sixty days of non-indulgence were enough to reverse the creeping effect, and succumbed once again to temptation.'

At this point Jekyll began to shudder violently and buried his face in his hands. That he had reached the end of his tether was painfully evident. After a moment, however, he steeled himself with visible effort and lowered his hands. The fire threw a shimmering red glow over his wasted features as he stared into it.

'The Edward Hyde who emerged after an imprisonment of two months was not the same corrupt but fun-loving fellow who went into it,' he continued. 'He was wild, totally unbridled. Hitherto he had tolerated Jekyll as a shelter and place of rest into which he could retreat after a night of frivolity; now he was consumed with hatred for the man whom he considered his gaoler, and for the entire *stratum* of society which he represented. His only goal was vengeance. Physically, he could not harm Jekyll without doing damage to himself as well, but he could strike back at him in other ways. If Hyde's weakness lay in his self-indulgence, Jekyll's was centred in conscience. Hyde knew that his excesses were a source of great disturbance to his other self; what better way to wreak his revenge than to commit a deed so foul that the doctor would never again be able to hold his head erect? I am familiar with his motives, you see, because whilst Jekyll and Hyde were two distinctly different individuals they still shared one memory.

'When Sir Danvers Carew, to whom Edward Hyde was a complete stranger, chanced to meet him during a stroll, tipped his hat, and politely asked for directions to a certain restaurant, my other self saw his opportunity and seized it. On that fateful night any who chose to speak to him would have been doomed – so great was his rage against all of mankind – but the very sight of this ancient and cultured gentleman and the cordial way in which he expressed himself, appearing to take no notice of the meanness of his chance acquaintance, stirred his fury to a fever pitch. He flew into a frenzy – but I will spare you the details, as they were recorded all too graphically in the next day's newspapers. Suffice it to say that Sir Danvers never stood a chance and that his life was as so much chaff beneath the madman's feet.

'What was Hyde's reaction, when the deed was done? Certainly not remorse. Panic was his strongest emotion. He looked round and, convinced that he was alone upon the path with the dead man, beat a hasty retreat to Soho, where he burnt those papers which linked him to Jekyll and from there fled to this address to take refuge in the body of one who was above suspicion.

'His revenge was complete, though self-destructive; for Jekyll, after the first seizure of guilt, renounced his double life. Symbolically, I crushed beneath my heel the key with which Hyde was wont to enter the laboratory section of the house, then informed Utterson — after handing him a farewell note to which I had forged Hyde's signature — that I was done with the fellow. Immediately thereafter I entered upon an intensive campaign to make up in some measure for Hyde's black existence. For the first time in years I resumed the mantle of physician, making charity cases my specialty. Thousands of pounds I donated anonymously towards the renovation of three of London's major hospitals. On a personal level, I rekindled old friendships, most notably with Hastie Lanyon, with whom I healed the breach which ten years ago had increased to the point where we no longer spoke. My every waking moment was devoted to improving my own little quarter of the world — a comedown, I grant you, from my youthful ideals of raising all of mankind to a new plane, but a more realistic course nonetheless, with more tangible results. It was both the least and the most I could do to atone for a crime for which I know now that there is no atonement. For the space of three months I was a contented man.

'Alas, it was that very contentment which led to my ruination. The pitfall to avoid when wearing sackcloth and ashes is that of assuming a false pride in one's nobility, which is contrary to its very meaning; I began to see myself in such pious terms, and for the first time in many weeks my thoughts wandered from my mission. I felt that the end of my self-imposed sentence was in view. An impure thought – that is all which was required. I was strolling in Regent's Park after a day of self-sacrifice when, without warning, and in less time that it takes to recount it, the transformation took place. Gone was Henry Jekyll, the physician and erstwhile scientist, respected and admired by all who knew him; in his place stood the murderer, Edward Hyde, whose scalp was worth thousands to the man fortunate enough to lay hands upon him.

'The horror of suddenly finding myself in a form which I had hoped never to assume again was gone in the instant of transformation. Blind panic replaced it. Hyde was miles from the safety of the laboratory in the midst of a city alive with constables. His description was known throughout the length and breadth of London. How to return? How to partake of the formula which was his sole salvation? In an instant the answer came: Lanyon! Final reconciliation between him and Jekyll had taken place over the dinner table only the night before. He who had refused the offer to aid the rash scientist three decades earlier might yet be won over. Through roundabout means Hyde made his way to shelter and drafted a note, signed by Jekyll: a certain drawer filled with chemicals in Jekyll's laboratory was to be brought to Lanyon's home until called for. Lanyon was to tell no-one, and even his servants were to be absent from the house at midnight, when the messenger was to be expected. The note was worded so desperately that no true Christian could refuse its plea. Hyde dispatched the letter and settled down impatiently to await midnight. At that hour – '

'I think that you have said enough, Doctor,' Holmes broke in. 'Lanyon's decline in health and subsequent death date from that night, when before his eyes the transformation took place.'

Jekyll nodded gravely. 'The temptation to reveal the secret to Jekyll's most ardent dissenter was too great. Jekyll would have practised restraint; Hyde cared only to demonstrate his triumph. I suppose that Lanyon's death is one more murder which may be attributed to me.

'It naturally follows that Jekyll's renewed isolation came about as a result of the uncertainty concerning when and where the change might take place.

'That is the horror of it, Mr. Holmes. It was an impurity in the powder which gave the potion its strength, an impurity which cannot be duplicated. I know, because I have tried every chemist in London. Without it I am doomed, for only by maintaining the utmost concentration am I allowed to remain in my present state. How swiftly tragedy can strike was demonstrated during your last visit, when I barely had time to turn you both from the room before the change occurred. Far from harming him, Hyde's crimes have given him dominance over his former master. At the same time they have sealed both our fates. Likely it is my despair over this revelation which has alarmed my servants.'

'Have you not attempted to analyse the powder to determine the nature of the impurity?' I asked.

'Attempted and failed, Doctor!' he cried. 'Surely your own medical training has made you aware of the infinity of matter which exists upon this planet, and of the utter hopelessness of any endeavour to identify a random substance whose properties do not conform to those of any within one man's limited experience.'

Holmes nodded. 'He is quite right, Watson. And even then, should he be fortunate enough, against all the laws of nature, to stumble upon the key to the mystery, the odds against his duplicating the exact ratio of the impurity to the base required to accomplish the desired effect are astronomical. One in twenty trillion would not seem too farfetched an equation. I am something of a dabbler in the chemical art myself, Dr. Jekyll,' he added modestly.

I smote my forehead. 'By thunder, that's right! I'd completely forgotten! Holmes! You're a chemist; where one man's knowledge has failed, another's may succeed. What say you, Doctor? Will you consent to have Sherlock Holmes examine the impurity?'

Again he shuddered. 'I had one remaining dose of the original powder; I consumed that just now. That is what I meant when I said that soon Jekyll will cease to be. Even now I fancy that I can hear Hyde's unearthly laughter echoing inside my skull. His triumph will be the end of us both.'

Even as he spoke, I imagined that I saw traces in Jekyll's features of that ghastly pallor which we had observed just before the termination of our last interview. I rose. I wanted to be gone before that transformation took place.

Holmes remained rooted before the fire. He studied our host with an air of clinical interest, as if he were a specimen on a card. 'One more mystery stands in need of a solution,' said he. 'Two months ago Hyde revealed himself in broad daylight near Lanyon's house. I know for a fact that he ventured out as Jekyll. Why did you take that risk?'

The scientist nodded. 'So it was you who pursued Hyde that day. He suspected as much, though he hardly recognized you.' He shrugged wearily. 'It was the madness of despair. I was obsessed suddenly with the notion that with Lanyon's brilliant assistance I might yet find some way to duplicate the original powder. The transformation *en route* brought me, or rather Hyde, to his senses and the rash hope was abandoned. The murderer's reappearance on Lanyon's doorstep might have prompted him to summon the police. He instructed the driver to return him to Jekyll's house, or rather round the corner from it, where he might gain entrance without the servants' seeing him. The conclusion came too late; by then Hyde had already been spotted.' He paused, then looked up with interest at my companion. 'What is it that has brought you here on this fateful day? Can it possibly be that in so short a space you were able to find the same truth which took me a lifetime?'

Holmes waved aside the question. 'A mere instinct. Something which I read earlier today came back to me over my violin. That, and something I witnessed this afternoon and failed to recognise for the final act of desperation that it was.'

A silence ensued which was as long and as heavy as that pall which settles over a room in which a corpse lies in state, seconds after the last mourner has filed out. Somewhere in the distance a clock ticked out Henry Jekyll's last moments in measured, emotionless beats.

Something akin to sympathy glimmered in the detective's normally cold eyes. 'What are your plans?'

'There is a phial of curare on the work-table. Jekyll has not the courage to use it; Hyde has not the will. I pray that he will choose it over the rope, which will certainly be his fate once he has been apprehended. There is no other direction in which he can flee.'

Holmes shook his head disapprovingly. 'Hyde will never commit suicide. His wicked self-love would demand that he find some other way to cheat the gallows.'

'Then there is but one alternative.'

As we watched, Jekyll pushed himself up and out of his chair and took up a poker from its place beside the fire. With it balanced in one hand he started towards the detective.

'What are you doing?' Holmes demanded. He fingered the revolver in his pocket.

'What a man who lacks both the will to live and the courage to die must do,' said the doctor, advancing with ponderous steps.

'Don't be a fool, Jekyll!' My companion retreated a step, exposing his weapon.

I raised my own. 'Look out, Holmes!' I cried. 'He's gone mad!'

Jekyll laughed then, a low, mirthless chuckle that convinced me that his mind had indeed become unsettled by his awful personal tragedy. 'No, Doctor,' said he, without slowing or taking his eyes from his intended victim. 'I really believe that I am thinking clearly for the first time in many, many months.'

Holmes had his back against the door now and could go no farther. Jekyll raised the poker high over his head and braced himself for the downswing. As he did so, his powerful frame, like a wax statuette placed too near an open hearth, seemed to shrivel until it resembled nothing other than Hyde's shrunken configuration. Holmes fired point-blank into his mid-section, once, twice.

For what seemed an eternity, his assailant stood as if paralysed, the rod poised over his head to deliver the fatal blow. I held my revolver steady and prepared to fire. Then Jekyll – Hyde, now – swayed and toppled, releasing the poker so that it fell with a clang to the floor. In the next instant he was sprawled on top of it. He shuddered and lay still.

I rushed forward and felt for a pulse. After a moment I looked up at my friend, who remained standing with his back to the door and the firearm smoking in his hand, and shook my head gravely.

'May God have mercy on his soul,' murmured Holmes.

There was a frantic knocking at the door.

'Jekyll!' It was Utterson's voice, taut with alarm. The doorknob rattled. 'Great Scott, Jekyll, if you're all right speak up! Down with the door, Poole!'

The door bucked in its frame as if a shoulder had slammed into it. Holmes was galvanized into action.

'Get over here, Watson!' he barked. 'Quickly! Hold the door!'

Putting up my pistol, I performed as bidden. I had no sooner placed my own shoulder against the door than my friend left it and dashed to Jekyll's worktable, which was heaped high with papers bearing notes and chemical symbols written in a close hand. He glanced at them briefly, then gathered them up in his arms and dumped them into a steel basin at his elbow. He then snatched up a bottle labeled 'Alcohol,' unstopped it, sniffed it to verify the contents, and upended it over the papers, soaking them thoroughly.

'Hurry, Holmes!' said I. A third party had joined Utterson and Poole on the other side of the door, and holding it against their combined efforts was taxing both my strength and the lock.

The detective stood back, struck a match, and tossed it into the bowl. Immediately the papers were engulfed in a sheet of flame that reached almost to the ceiling.

'And with Jekyll's notes go the chances of anyone ever repeating his diabolical experiments,' said he, watching the conflagration as it consumed the hopes and dreams of that misguided unfortunate, Henry Jekyll. 'You may come away from the door now, Watson.'

His final words were all but drowned out as the heavy door splintered beneath the blow of an axe.

Twenty

ADVICE FOR MR. STEVENSON

One day towards the close of spring I returned to Baker Street after a morning spent over the billiard table at my club to find Sherlock Holmes deep in conversation with a man whose features I could not see, seated as he was with his back to the door. Excusing myself, I was backing out to leave them in peace when Holmes hailed me and waved me back inside.

'You might wish to meet our visitor, Watson,' said he, rising. 'As fellow writers, you have much in common. Mr. Robert Louis Stevenson, allow me to present Dr. Watson.'

I gazed with interest at the man who rose and turned to face me, extending his hand. I would have placed his age at forty, but in fact he was several years younger. Slight of build, he wore his black hair long and parted to one side and sported a drooping moustache which concealed the corners of pallid lips. His eyes were deep-set and melancholy, his face gaunt as that of my fellow-lodger and nearly as pale. He seemed sickly, and though his grip was firm I received the impression that he was not naturally robust. The black frockcoat he wore served only to heighten the funereal effect of his appearance.

'You are familiar with the name of Stevenson,' said Holmes with a mischievous twinkle in his eye. 'He is the man who penned that story from which you enthusiastically read extracts for my benefit some months ago, the one about pirates and pieces of eight.'

'Treasure Island!' I cried, and fell to pumping our astonished visitor's hand until his sallow cheeks flushed with embarrassment. 'Robert Louis Stevenson, of course! My congratulations upon a fine example of story-telling. When Jim Hawkins encounters Ben Gunn –'

'Enough, Watson, enough!' chuckled Holmes. 'It's plain that you are causing our guest discomfort. He has come not to talk of past triumphs but to lay the groundwork for his next literary effort. I have been filling him in upon the details of our recent adventure with the late Henry Jekyll and his unlamented companion, Edward Hyde.'

'That is correct,' said our visitor, in whose cultured speech I thought that I detected a trace of an American accent. He indicated a notebook lying open upon the arm of the chair in which he had seen sitting, its pages filled with closely-written script. 'After substantial argument I have persuaded Mr. Holmes to provide me with a fairly complete account of the affair. I hope to publish it in the form of a case history after I have spoken with one or two of the other principals involved.'

I looked at Holmes in reproach. He shrugged.

'My dear fellow, do not be disheartened. I have betrayed no trust which has not already been betrayed. Too many at Whitehall were privy to the secret. It was bound to be leaked by someone sooner or later. I have been unable to convince Mr. Stevenson that he knew quite as much about the affair as I did when he arrived.'

'Concerning the facts, yes.' agreed the other. 'But the personal slant was missing. Mr. Holmes has been gracious enough to supply that essential ingredient. I have nearly enough now to begin writing.'

'A most bizarre episode,' I commented, repressing a shudder at the memory of recent events. The newspapers had only just ceased carrying eulogies for the departed Henry Jekyll, who was interred late in March following a simple service over his closed casket. At the time, it was said, pallbearers had commented upon the surprising lightness of the receptacle as they were carrying it down the steps of the church.

'I quite agree. Mr. Holmes's version of the story proved most enlightening. He is a remarkable man. Do you know that he divined without my telling him that I had spent a great deal of time in the American West, particularly round San Francisco? Something about my speech. I think that I shall have no difficulty making him the hero of my account.'

Holmes held up a hand. 'I am afraid that I cannot allow you to do that, Mr. Stevenson. No, no – hear me out. There is a serious possibility that the law, particularly a certain Scotland Yard Inspector of my acquaintance, will accuse me of withholding evidence if my name is allowed to appear in any active capacity. There is also the little matter of my having killed a man, and self-defence or no, I am far too busy at the moment to waste my time engaging in idle banter with some barrister at the Assizes. Newcomen was angry enough when I did not make good on my promise to provide him with a solution by the end of March; I would rather not rub salt into wounds which are still raw. I have your own reputation in mind as well, for any mention of Dr. Watson or myself would automatically establish yours as an account of an actual event, and I have already decided that no-one is going to believe you. You would spare yourself much pain if you published it as fiction and left us out of it. The tale is entertaining enough to assure you a permanent place in literature, but as a documentary it rings much too fancifully and could expose you to ridicule. I commend to you, sir, the writing of a thriller which will captivate the world, but to let what is past remain in the past. You would be doing both the world and yourself a very great favour.'

Throughout this monologue, Stevenson's expression changed from one of bewilderment to protest, from protest to dismay, and finally as the validity of Sherlock Holmes's argument became clear, to grudging acquiescence.

'But how shall I go about it?' he demanded. 'I can alter the facts to say that Jekyll fulfilled his intention to poison himself, but that is only one problem among many. What shall I tell my readers when they ask me where I got my inspiration?'

The detective smiled, and again the mischievous light danced in his grey eyes. 'You are the writer; use your imagination. Tell them you dreamt it.'

Robert Louis Stevenson forgot himself so far as to smile at this pleasantry, but it was evident by the thoughtful look upon his face that his imaginative brain was already at work. And when, some months later, his account swept the reading public by storm and it came time to explain to a curious world where he obtained such an intriguing idea, I was not very much surprised to learn that he had not forgotten the advice which Sherlock Holmes had given him.

ACKNOWLEDGEMENTS

If we are to accept the evidence of recent book lists, which fairly shudder beneath the weight of "newly discovered" titles by John H. Watson, M.D., it would appear that the good doctor wrote a great deal more than he published, and was in fact one of the most prolific authors of his or any other time. The very limits of human nature insist that he could not have penned *all* of them, and it naturally follows that many are forgeries, a situation that has made the going difficult for those few which, for lack of evidence to the contrary, must be considered genuine. Such was the case with *Sherlock Holmes vs. Dracula: Or the Adventure of the Sanguinary Count*, and I harbor no illusions that the present volume does not face a journey equally as demanding.

Thus it became doubly important that I check and crosscheck each of the manuscript's dubious points as it arose, that I might arm myself against the brickbats that the unbelieving would hurl my way as surely as Tonga the Andamanese spat poison-tipped darts at Holmes, Watson, and Athelney Jones during the chase sequence in *The Sign of Four*. I am therefore indebted to the following works for their safe and sure guidance through the mine field of Sherlockiana and Victoriana: *The Annotated Sherlock Holmes*, by William S. Baring-Gould; *Sherlock Holmes of Baker Street*, also by Baring-Gould; *In the Footsteps of Sherlock Holmes*, by Michael Harrison; *The Private Life of Sherlock Holmes*, by Vincent Starrett; *The Encyclopaedia Sherlockiana*, by Jack Tracy; and *Naked Is the Best Disguise*, by Samuel Rosenberg, the last of which was of no practical help at all in authenticating the manuscript, but whose out-landishly entertaining leaps to various conclusions concerning the relationship of Watson's writing to the private and political opinions of Sir Arthur Conan Doyle, his literary agent, helped keep aflame my interest in things Sherlockian.

For those who wish to delve further into the events contained between these covers, I heartily recommend *The Strange Case of Dr. Jekyll and Mr. Hyde*, by Robert Louis Stevenson. As a tale of terror, mystery, and tragedy it is hard to beat, and is one to which Hollywood has yet to do justice.

Finally, many thanks are due once again to William B. Thompson, a friend of long standing, for his spiritual support, the Arcadia Mixture, Ann Arbor scion of the Baker Street Irregulars, for comic relief, and to Sherlockians everywhere, latent and overt, for their continuing interest in the exploits of the world's first consulting detective, and, as always, my family, because they are my family.

DR. JEKYLL'S "CASE OF IDENTITY": A WORD AFTER BY LOREN D. ESTELMAN

This is the one Hollywood didn't like.

Too cerebral, they said; not at all like its predecessor, *Sherlock Holmes vs. Dracula, or The Adventure of the Sanguinary Count.* (Never mind that they didn't make that one, either.) Not enough slam-bang action, no midnight crypt visits, no caped vampires carrying off swooning females in diaphanous negligees, and only one special effect. Nothing that would translate into big box-office, like Ben's trained rats or the pea-soup projectile vomiting of Linda Blair in *The Exorcist.* Just Robert Louis Stevenson's original vision restored, along with his subtextual commentary on late-Victorian hypocrisy, with the greatest detective who never lived folded into the mixture.

I wasn't disappointed. Movie action on *Sherlock Holmes vs. Dracula* had stalled, thanks mostly to the difficult people who were then representing the Sir Arthur Conan Doyle estate and who had insisted on entertainment negotiation rights and a whopping share of the proceeds therefrom; it was clear that if there was to be a motion picture about Holmes and Dracula, it would not be based on my book. Since

Dr. Jekyll and Mr. Holmes had received its sanction on the same terms, I wasn't investing in sun block and a ticket to the Coast.

The reaction from the studios did, however, teach me something about the philosophy of film. Screenwriting is a limited art, circumscribed by the writer's inability to climb inside the minds of his characters. Barring the creaky, overused technique of the voiceover, a character's personality can be revealed only through action: Man kicks dog – villain; man rescues kitten – hero. The sight of Dracula sucking blood is not a positive character reference, but the tableau of Holmes advancing upon the vampire with crucifix in hand would qualify him for high office.

Dr. Jekyll and Mr. Holmes would not play onscreen for the very reason that makes it unique in the world of the action-suspense yarn: it presents a man of intellect retracing the steps of another man of intellect through the labyrinth of the human mind. Bereft of physical evidence – telltale footprints, broken pen-points – Holmes is forced to track the vanished Jekyll's movements through the books he studied in his quest for the cause and cure of personal evil. Andy Warhol may have contented himself with filming reel after reel of a man bent over a tome of science or philosophy, nothing moving but the pages and the smoke drifting up from the bowl of his pipe; Steven Spielberg (or more likely, Roger Corman or Joel Schumacher) may not. The greatest advantage enjoyed by the writer of fiction intended to be read is also the biggest roadblock to adaptation to the screen.

Stevenson presented *The Strange Case of Dr. Jekyll and Mr. Hyde* as a mystery, with Henry Jekyll's lawyer, the dour Utterson, performing as detective. Until Edward Hyde's suicide and the subsequent discovery of Hastie Lanyon's posthumous narrative and Jekyll's journal, the loathsome Hyde's hold over respectable Henry Jekyll is kept from the reader. Time and the novella's fame (people who have never read Stevenson and are unaware of the story and the many motion pictures that have been based upon it know immediately what is meant by the phrase "Jekyll and Hyde") have rendered the mystery angle superfluous. As early as its first appearance on the Victorian stage, the tale was told in linear fashion, beginning with the medical man's experiments and his first transformation and finishing with his demise. Every film version to date has followed that formula (appropriate word) as if the studios elected to option the deceased doctor's journal over the Stevenson treatment.

But Sherlock Holmes is a detective. As such, his entry was dictated by convenience and reason to coincide with Utterson's concern about the singular terms of his client's will. All that follows is as Stevenson envisioned, albeit with a Doylesque twist and an ending more in keeping with the proactive role of the sleuth as hero. (More on that ending later; like the classic itself, the first incarnation bore little resemblance to the last.)

It's been said that a trained researcher can deduce the nature of a pond by an examination of a single drop of water. Likewise a child of the twenty-first century, with no knowledge of the nineteenth, will someday be able to comprehend the surface and subterranean details of late-Victorian English society on the basis of a first-time reading of *Dr. Jekyll and Mr. Hyde.* Only Oscar Wilde's *Picture of Dorian Gray* and H. G. Wells's *The Invisible Man* came as close during the period to capturing the central *angst* of a civilization at odds with its own ideal.

All times are repressed. From the tyrannical Puritanism of Cromwell to the pressures exerted by the religious right and the politically correct left under Clinton, the artist has repeatedly been forced to fly in the face of a sanctimonious majority in the service of truth. The example of the widowed Queen Victoria demanded that drawing-room manners and public-school concepts of honor and fair play be exhibited on all occasions, while the evidence of her many children indicated a variety of pleasures in the bedchamber, courtesy of the late Prince Consort.

The dream thus personified was to maintain one's social standing without neglecting the baser appetites; to misbehave gloriously and with impunity. Let Dorian's likeness display the physical signs of his debauchery to a sealed room while its original turned the unlined face of an angel to the world. Permit Jekyll to practice good works for the admiration of his colleagues, and Hyde to taste the smorgasbord of sordid delights to be found in the East End. It's the wish-dream of every pubescent schoolboy who longs to be invisible so he can enter and exit the girls' locker-room at will.

How natural, then, that the ultra-conservative John H. Watson — wounded war veteran, incorruptible physician, loyal companion — and the Bohemian Sherlock Holmes — student of human frailty, bemused cynic, abuser of drugs and alcohol — should find themselves drawn into the two halves of Jekyll's world. The detective will not hesitate to follow the spoor through opium dens and brothels. The doctor will trail him reluctantly, but act with decision to snatch his friend back onto safe ground should his eagerness precipitate him over the edge of the abyss. It was not unique territory for this partnership: "A Case of Identity" and "The Man With the Twisted Lip" had profound things to say about double lives and subsumed personalities. And as they had been with Dracula's invasion of Holmes's London, the time and setting made the prospect of a summit inevitable.

First and foremost, I am an entertainer, not an academic. I'm incapable of allowing any tale to remain sedentary. The insertion of the frenetic hansom cab chase in Chapter Eleven, with its toppling peddlers' carts and mud-splattered policemen, earned favorable comments from reviewers — jaded by the influx of Sherlockian pastiches post-Nicholas Meyer's *The Seven-Percent Solution* — for its humor and originality. I humbly accept the compliment of hilarity, but as for being a prime mover I must pass that credit on to the kings of silent comedy whose work inspired the scene. I suspect the *maestri* Keaton and Chaplin would have found an appreciative audience in both Holmes and Watson, one for the precision of the stunt direction, the other for the *schtik*.

Dr. Jekyll and Mr. Holmes is not as well known as *Sherlock Holmes vs. Dracula*; the latter remained in print without interruption for twenty years, and has appeared twice since, with only brief periods of unavailability. This publication marks the latter's first solo appearance since the Penguin reissue in 1980. The difference has to do with the vast following claimed by Holmes and Dracula individually, while the Stevenson *ménage* has yet to achieve cult status. Yet I consider *Dr. Jekyll and Mr. Holmes* the better book. It's a more mature work, the Sherlockian rhythms are more faithful to the model, and the title is superior. *Sherlock Holmes vs. Dracula* still sounds too much like a film directed by Edward Wood, Jr. I only settled on it because I couldn't think of a better way to get the names of both hot-button characters up front.

Not everyone at Doubleday & Co. agreed with me. One of the mental giants in sales and marketing wanted to call the book *Sherlock Holmes and Dr. Jekyll and Mr. Hyde*, on the theory that bred-in-the-bone Sherlockians looked up all pastiches under "S" in *Books in Print*. I ignored the twerp.

I placed more faith in the suggestion of my editor, Cathleen Jordan, that my original ending – Jekyll/Hyde committing suicide while Holmes and Watson look on – added nothing to Stevenson's and relegated the detective and his amanuensis to the roles of passive witnesses. The present conclusion, in which the pitiable schizophrenic forces Holmes to put him out of his misery (or *them* out of *their* misery), preserves Jekyll's tragic heroism while making Holmes's part in it more dynamic. The only editorial complaint, as I recall, was that the new ending added twenty pages to the narrative. Consider it the author's equivalent of a director's cut.

The thing that has vexed me most about all previous published editions is they contained the same egregious typo in the last line of Watson's narrative. As written, in regard to Holmes's directive to Stevenson to leave Holmes and Watson out of his account of the Jekyll case, it read: "I was not very much surprised to learn that he had not forgotten the advice which Sherlock Holmes had given him." As published in the first Doubleday edition, it read: "I was not surprised to learn that he had forgotten the advice which Sherlock Holmes had given him." The deletion of that second *not* made nonsense of the crucial last line and negated the entire premise, suggesting as it did that Holmes and Watson *had* appeared in the Stevenson version, rendering *Dr. Jekyll and Mr. Holmes* redundant. Despite editorial promises to correct the error in future printings, it cropped up in every edition published by Doubleday, Penguin, and the Book-of-the-Month Club. The copy you hold is thus the first to contain the correct ending.

Literary legend has it that Stevenson wrote the first version of *Jekyll* in a delirious three days, under the influence of a nightmare, only to destroy it upon being told by his wife that he had overlooked the story's mythic potential in favor of creating a lowbrow "crawler." The version he then wrote is the one which has come down to us. Under the influence of my own premise, I wondered if perhaps the story I sat down to tell was the one Holmes had persuaded Stevenson to abandon. Con men and writers of fiction are equally susceptible to their own pitches.

There is a popular misconception, circulated by critics and scholars who should know better, that the characters created by Sir Arthur Conan Doyle passed into public domain some time ago. They are still very much in the control of those who administer his estate. The death-plus-thirty-years rule that governed British copyright law protected all rights worldwide until 1980, but the dates of publication in *Collier's* of the later Sherlock Holmes stories continued to shield the characters of

Holmes and Watson in the United States until 2000. In the meantime, an international copyright law was passed stating that literary creations will remain the property of a writer's estate until seventy years after death. The ghost of Sir Arthur is still to be reckoned with; a situation with which I have no problem, except for migraines caused by some of the people I have had to placate. Dame Jean Doyle-Bromet, daughter of Sir Arthur, was a treasure. A number of the supernumeraries who have claimed to speak for her, before her death and after, are disinterred findings of a different type.

My first agent, the late Ray Puechner, bore the brunt of these associations, and confided to me that he had never come closer to quitting Alcoholics Anonymous than he did during and after conferences attendant to receiving permission to publish *Sherlock Holmes vs. Dracula*. The opinions of the editors at Doubleday were similar. Cathleen Jordan wrote me that when all the feathers had settled and then *Dr. Jekyll and Mr. Holmes* landed on her desk, with its promise of more confrontations to come, she had to go out for a long walk before she could bring herself to read the manuscript. She liked it enough to join hands once again with Ray and walk back into the Valley of Fear.

My next project was *Motor City Blue*, the first Amos Walker mystery, but I would not tell Ray what it was about. In those days I didn't discuss ongoing work, believing that a negative comment would halt my momentum. After the trouble with the guardians of Conan Doyle's characters, however, I felt compelled to assure him it was not a story involving Sherlock Holmes or Dr. Watson or Professor Moriarty or any of that lot. Ray's reply: "If the new one is a Professor Challenger story, I'll kill you."

Afterword first published in the 2001 edition.

JOHN. H. WATSON, M.D., M.B., B.S., M.R.C.S., was born in England in 1852, and was friend, confidant, and chronicler of the great detective, Mr. Sherlock Holmes, whose exploits have served to inspire generations of amateur sleuths around the world since its first publication in the *Strand* magazine in the late 1890s. In 1878 he took his medical degree at the University of London and shortly after served as assistant surgeon with the Fifth Northumberland Fusiliers in Afghanistan. There he transferred to the Berkshires, and was severely wounded in the Battle of Maiwand, after which he left the service and returned to London. While there, he began his long association with Sherlock Holmes, who became the subject of his more than sixty published books and articles. Dr. Watson died in 1940.

LOREN D. ESTLEMAN is a graduate of Eastern Michigan University and a veteran police-court journalist. Since the publication of his first novel in 1976, he has established himself as a leading writer of both mystery and western fiction. His western novels include Golden Spur Award winner *Aces and Eights*, *Mister St. John*, *The Stranglers*, and *Gun Man*. His Amos Walker, Private Eye series includes *Motor City Blue*, *Angel Eyes*, *The Midnight Man*, *The Glass Highway*, Shamus Award-winner *Sugartown*, *Every Brilliant Eye*, *Lady Yesterday*, *Downriver*, and *A Smile on the Face of the Tiger*. Mr. Estleman lives in Michigan with his wife, Deborah, who writes under the name Deborah Morgan.

Also Available

the further adventures of

SHERLOCK HOLMES

THE WHITECHAPEL HORRORS

by

EDWARD B. HANNA

One

~~~

"It is not really difficult to construct a series of inferences, each
dependent upon its predecessor and each simple in itself."
— *The Adventure of the Dancing Men*

"A perfectly marvelous, gruesome experience," observed Sherlock
Holmes brightly as he and Watson wended their way through the
crowds streaming out of the theater into the gaiety and glare of the gaslit
Strand. "I cannot thank you enough for insisting that I accompany you
this evening, Watson. Rarely have I been witness to a more dramatic
transformation of good to evil, either onstage or off, than our American
friend has so ably portrayed for us."

He pondered for a while as they walked, his sharp profile silhouetted
against the glow of light. It was the first of September, the night was
warm and clinging, the myriad smells of the city an almost palpable
presence. London, noisy, noisome, nattering London: aged, ageless,
dignified, eccentric in her ways — seat of Empire, capital of all the world;
that indomitable gray lady of drab aspect but sparkling personality —

was at her very, very best and most radiant. And Holmes, ebullient and uncommonly chatty, was in a mood to match.

"I have no doubt the author was telling us," he said after a time, "that we are all capable of such a transformation. Or, should I say transmogrification? – such a wonderful word, don't you think? – capable of it even without the benefit of a remarkable chemical potion; that we all, each and every one of us, have the capacity for good and evil – the capability of performing both good works and ill – and precious little indeed is required to lead us down one path or the other. While hardly an original thought, it is sobering nonetheless."

But if he found the notion sobering, it was not for very long. He was in particularly buoyant spirits, having just the previous day brought about a successful conclusion to the amusing affair concerning Mrs. Cecil Forrester. And if his hawklike features seemed even sharper than usual, the cheekbones more pronounced, the piercing eyes the more deepset, it was due to an unusually busy period for him, one of the busiest of his career, when case seemed to follow demanding case, one on top of the other, with hardly a day between that was free from tension and strenuous mental effort. Though the pace had taken its toll insofar as his physical appearance was concerned – he was even thinner, more gaunt than ever, and his complexion a shade or two paler – it did nothing to sap his energy or weaken his powers. It was obvious to those who knew him – Watson in particular, who knew him best – that he not only thrived on the activity, but positively reveled in it, was invigorated by it. As nature abhorred a vacuum, he was fond of saying, he could not tolerate inactivity.

Still, Watson was glad to have been able to entice him away from Baker Street for a few hours of diversion and relaxation. Left to his own devices, Holmes would have been content to remain behind, indeed would have preferred it, cloistered like a hermit amid his index books and papers and chemical paraphernalia, the violin his only diversion, cherrywood and shag his only solace.

Several theaters seemed to be emptying out at once along the Strand, and the street was rapidly filling with even greater throngs of gentlemen in crisp evening dress and fashionably gowned women, their laughter and chatter vying with the entreaties of the flower girls and the urgent cries of the newsboys working the crowd.

"'Ave a flower for yer button'ole, guv? 'Ave a loverly flower?"

"Murder! Another foul murder in the East End! 'Ere, read the latest!"

"Nice button'ole, sir? Take some nice daffs 'ome for the missus?"

Holmes and Watson elbowed their way through the crowd with increasing difficulty, conversation made impossible by the press and clamor around them.

"Here, Watson, we will never get a cab in all this. Let us make our way to Simpson's and wait for the crowds to dissipate."

"Capital idea, I'm famished," Watson shot back, dodging a pinched-faced little girl with a huge flower basket crooked in her arm.

Holmes led the way, stopping momentarily to snatch up a selection of evening newspapers from grimy hands. Then the pair of them, holding on to their silk hats against the crush, forced their way through to the curb and navigated the short distance to the restaurant, gratefully entering through etched-glass doors into an oasis of potted palms and marble columns, ordered, calm, genteel murmurings, and starched white napery.

It was not long before they were ushered to a table, despite several parties of late diners waiting to be seated; for the eminent Mr. Holmes and his companion were not unknown to the manager, Mr. Crathie, who ruled his domain with a majesty and manner the czar himself would have envied. Shortly after taking their places, they were served a light supper of smoked salmon and capers, accompanied by a frosty bottle of hock.

Conversation between the two old friends was minimal, even monosyllabic, but there was nothing awkward about it or strained, merely a comfortable absence of talk. Small talk was anathema to Holmes in any case, but the two had known each other for so long, and were so accustomed to each other's company, the mere physical presence of the other was enough to satisfy any need for human companionship. Communication between them was all but superfluous in any case, their respective opinions on almost any subject being well known to the other. And besides, throughout most of the meal Holmes had his face buried in one or the other of his precious newspapers, punctuating the columns of type as he scanned them with assorted sniffs and grunts and other sounds of disparagement occasionally interspersed with such muttered editorial comments as "Rubbish!" "What nonsense!" and, for variety's sake, an occasional cryptic and explosive "*Hah!*"

Watson, well used to Holmes's eccentric ways, resolutely ignored him, content to occupy his time by idly observing the passing scene. The captain and waiters, on the other hand, could not ignore him: An untidy pile of discarded newspapers was piling up at his feet, and they were in somewhat of a quandary over what to do about it. Holmes, of course, was totally oblivious to it all.

"It would seem," he said finally, laying aside the last of the journals with a final grunt of annoyance as their coffee was served – "It would seem that our friends at Scotland Yard have their work cut out for them."

"Oh?" responded Watson with an air of disinterest. "What are they up to now?"

Holmes looked at him quizzically from across the table, an amused smile on his thin lips. "Murder! Murder most foul! Really, Watson! Surely you are not so completely unobservant that you failed to take note of the cries of the news vendors as we left the theater. The street is fairly ringing with their voices! 'Orrible murder in Whitechapel,'" he mimicked. "'Sco'ln' Yard w'out a clue.'"

Watson made a face. "Well, I hadn't noticed, actually. But surely, Holmes, neither bit of information is hardly unusual. There must be a dozen murders in that section of the city every week, and few if any are ever solved: You above all people must be aware of that. What makes this one any different?"

"If the popular press are to be believed —" He broke off in midsentence and laughed. "What a silly premise to go on, eh? Still, if there is even a shred of truth to their rather lurid accounts, this particular murder contains features that are not entirely devoid of interest. But what intrigues me more, Watson — what intrigues me infinitely more at the moment — is your astounding ability to filter from your mind even the most obvious and urgent of external stimuli. It's almost as if you have an insulating wall around you, a magical glass curtain through which you can be seen and heard but out of which you cannot see or hear! Is this a talent you were born with, old chap, or have you cultivated it over the years? Trained yourself through arduous study and painstaking application?"

"Really, Holmes, you exaggerate," Watson replied defensively. He was both hurt by Holmes's sarcastic rebuke and just a little annoyed.

"Do I? Do I indeed? Well, let us try a little test, shall we? Take, for example, the couple sitting at the table to my left and slightly behind me. You've been eyeing the young lady avidly enough during our meal. I deduce that it is the low cut of her gown that interests you, for her facial beauty is of the kind that comes mostly from the paint pot and is not of the good, simple English variety that usually attracts your attention. What can you tell me about the couple in general?"

Watson glanced over Holmes's shoulder. "Oh, that pretty little thing with the auburn hair — the one with the stoutish, balding chap, eh?"

"Yaas," Holmes drawled, the single word heavy with sarcasm. He examined his fingernails. "The wealthy American couple, just come over from Paris on the boat-train without their servants. He's in railroads, in the western regions of the United States, I believe, but has spent no little time in England. They are waiting – he, rather impatiently, anxiously – for a third party to join them, a business acquaintance, no doubt – one who is beneath their station but of no small importance to them in any event."

Watson put down his cup with a clatter. "Really, Holmes! *Really!*" he sputtered. "There is no possible way you could know all that. Not even you! This time you have gone too far."

"Have I indeed? Your problem, dear chap, as I have had occasion to remind you, is that you see but do not observe; you hear but do not listen. For a literary man, Watson – and note that I do not comment on the merit of your latest account of my little problems – for a man with the pretenses of being a writer, you are singularly unobservant. Honestly, sometimes I am close to despair."

He removed a cigarette from his case with a flourish and paused for the waiter to light it, a mischievous glint in his eye.

Watson gave him a sidelong look. "Very well, Holmes, I will nibble at your lure. Pray explain yourself!"

Holmes threw back his head and laughed. "But it is so very simple. As I have told you often enough, one has only to take note of the basic facts. For example, a mere glance will tell you that this particular couple is not only wealthy, but extremely wealthy. Their haughty demeanor, the quality of their clothes, the young lady's jewelry, and the gentleman's rather large diamond ring on the little finger of his left hand would suffice to tell you that. The ring also identifies our man as American: A 'pinky ring,' I believe it is called. What Englishman of breeding would ever think of wearing one of those?"

Holmes drew on his cigarette and continued, the exhalation of smoke intermingling with his dissertation. "That they are recently come from Paris is equally apparent: The lady is wearing the very latest in Parisian fashion – the low decolletage is, I believe, as decidedly French as it is delightfully revealing – and the fabric of the gown is obviously quite new, stiff with newness, probably never worn before. That they arrived this very evening is not terribly difficult to ascertain. Their clothes are somewhat creased, you see. Fresh out of the steamer trunk. Obviously, their appointment at Simpson's is of an urgent nature, otherwise they would have taken the time to have the hotel valet remove the creases before changing into the garments. That they are traveling without personal servants can be deduced by the simple fact that the gentleman's sleeve links, while similar, are mismatched, and the lady's hair, while freshly brushed, is not so carefully coiffed as one might expect it to be. No self-respecting manservant or lady's maid would permit their master or mistress to go out of an evening in such a state, not if they value their positions and take pride in their calling."

Watson sighed, a resigned expression on his face. He smoothed his mustache with his hand, a gesture of exasperation. "And the rest? How did you deduce all of that, dare I ask?"

"Oh, no great mystery, really. The man's suit of clothes is obviously Savile Row from the cut; custom made from good English cloth. It is not new. Ergo, he has visited our blessed plot before, at least once and for a long enough stay to have at least one suit, probably three or four, made to measure."

"Three or four? You know that with certainty, do you?"

Holmes, who was fastidious in his dress and surprisingly fashion conscious, and the possessor of an extensive wardrobe now that his success permitted it, allowed a slightly patronizing tone to color his reply.

"Formal attire would usually be a last selection; an everyday frock coat or 'Prince Albert' and more casual garments for traveling and for weekend country wear would customarily be the first, second, and third choices."

Watson looked pained, but he bravely, perhaps foolishly, continued: "You said he was a railroad man. How do you come by that, eh? And your conjecture that he is waiting for an urgent appointment, a business engagement, you said — and with someone beneath his station? How do you arrive at those conclusions?" He snorted. "Admit it, Holmes: pure guesswork, plain and simple!"

"You know me better than that," Holmes said, casually dabbing at his lips with a napkin. "I never guess." His lips puckered in a prim smile.

"Well then?" said Watson impatiently, drumming his fingers on the table.

"It is manifestly clear that the gentleman is waiting for another individual because of his repeated glances toward the door — anxious glances which suggest that the other party is not only eagerly awaited, but of no small importance to the gentleman in question. That it is one individual and not more is supported by the obvious fact (so obvious, Watson) that the gentleman and lady are seated at a table for four, and there is only one other place setting in evidence. These conclusions are all supported by the additional observations that the man and his charming companion — his wife, I dare say, from his inattentive manner — have yet to order from the menu despite being at table for some considerable time, and the wretched fellow is well into at least his third whiskey and soda — with ice, I might add," he said with a slight curl to the lip, "further evidence he is an American, should any be needed."

"As for the rest —" Holmes stubbed his cigarette out and continued: "That the man has a well-stuffed leather briefcase on the chair beside him suggests an engagement of a business nature. Why else would anyone bring such an encumbrance to a late evening supper? As for the engagement being with someone beneath his station..." Holmes sighed and gave Watson a somewhat patronizing look. "Really, Watson, this is getting tiresome. Obviously, our friends over there are wealthy enough to dine at the Ritz or the Cafe Monico. Why Simpson's, as good as it is, with its simple English fare? Hardly what a wealthy American tourist or business magnate would choose unless he had good and sufficient reason to do so – such as not wishing to appear in a highly fashionable restaurant that caters to the *crème* of society with someone unsuitably dressed or of a lower station."

Watson raised his hands in a gesture of surrender. "Enough, enough; I should have known better than to doubt you. You have my most abject apologies. Now, for God's sake let us get the bill and find our way home. I am suddenly very weary and want only my bed."

Holmes chuckled and snapped his fingers for the waiter.

As they threaded their way toward the entrance minutes later, Watson had to step to one side to avoid colliding with a man rushing headlong into the restaurant: a short, round individual with a large mustache, who after a hurried glance around the room made directly for the table occupied by the couple in question, profuse with apologies once having arrived. He was carrying a bulky briefcase and was dressed in a sagging dark business suit, not of the best cut or material. His voice, which could be clearly heard over the hubbub of the restaurant, had a decidedly middle-class accent – *lower* middle class. Watson shot Holmes a sidelong glance to see if he had noticed. He need not have bothered: Holmes's face was a mask of perfect innocence. There was just the glimmer of a smile, the mere hint of a smile on his thin lips, nothing more.

"We have a visitor, Holmes," said Watson as their hansom clattered to a halt in front of their lodgings. There was a light in their sitting room window, the shadow of a human form in evidence.

"I am not totally surprised," said Holmes laconically.

"You were expecting someone at this late hour?"

"No, not really. Nor am I surprised someone is here. H-Division, in all likelihood." Without a further word of explanation he bounded from the cab, his eyes bright with anticipation, leaving Watson to settle the fare and follow.

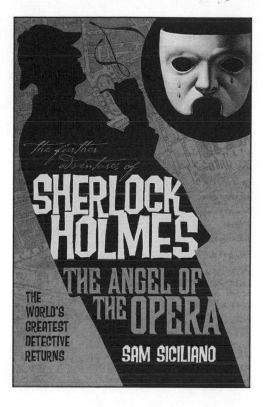

THE FURTHER ADVENTURES
OF SHERLOCK HOLMES
THE ANGEL OF THE OPERA

Sam Siciliano

Paris 1890: Sherlock Holmes is called across the English Channel to the famous
Opera House, where he is challenged to discover the true motivations and secrets of
the notorious Phantom who rules its depths with passion and defiance.

ISBN: 9781848568617

AVAILABLE MARCH 2011

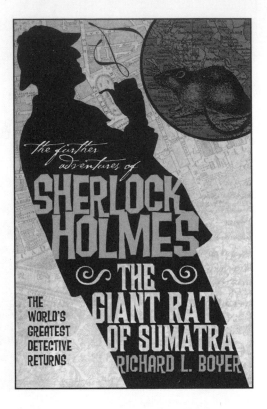

THE FURTHER ADVENTURES
OF SHERLOCK HOLMES

THE GIANT RAT OF SUMATRA

Richard L. Boyer

For many years, Dr Watson kept the tale of The Giant Rat of Sumatra a secret.
However, before he died, he arranged that the strange story of the giant rat should
be held in the vaults of a London bank until all the protagonists were dead...

ISBN: 9781848568600

AVAILABLE MARCH 2011